ISSN 2333-9284

Writing Texas

2013-14

I0684491

Edited by

Julie Chappell
Marilyn Robitaille

Writing Texas contains some of the fiction, poetry, and nonfiction presented at the annual meeting of the Texas Association of Creative Writing Teachers.

TACWT is a community of secondary and higher education teachers and professors, workshop facilitators, students, and individual writers. Much of the organization's work focuses on proliferating literary arts in Texas.

www.writingtexas.org
www.tacwt.org

LAMAR UNIVERSITY Press

Also from Lamar University Press

Jean Andrews, *High Tides, Low Tides: the Story of Leroy Colombo*
Alan Berecka, *With Our Baggage*
*David Bowles, *Flower, Song, Dance: Aztec and Mayan Poetry*
*Jerry Bradley, *Crownfeathers and Effigies*
Robert Murray Davis, *Levels of Incompetence: An Academic Life*
*William Virgil Davis, *The Bones Poems*
*Jeffrey Delotto, *Voices Writ in Sand*
Gerald Duff, *Memphis Mojo*
Mimi Ferebee, *Wildfires and Atmospheric Memories*
Ken Hada, *Margaritas and Redfish*
Michelle Hartman, *Disenchanted and Disgruntled*
*Lynn Hoggard, *Motherland, Stories and Poems from Louisiana*
Dominique Inge, *A Garden on the Brazos*
*Gretchen Johnson, *The Joy of Deception*
*Gretchen Johnson, *A Trip Through Downer, Minnesota*
Christopher Linforth, *When You Find Us We Will Be Gone*
Tom Mack and *Andrew Geyer, editors, *A Shared Voice*
Dave Oliphant, *The Pilgrimage, Selected Poems: 1962-2012*
*Janet McCann, *The Crone at the Casino*
Erin Murphy, *Ancilla*
*Harold Raley, *Louisiana Rogue*
*Carol Coffee Reposa, *Underground Musicians*
*Jim Sanderson, *Trashy Behavior*
*Jan Seale, *Appearances*
*Jan Seale, *The Parkinson Poems*
Melvin Sterne, *The Number You Have Reached*

for more information go to
www.LamarUniversityPress.Org

*member of TACWT

ISBN: 978-0-9911074-0-7

From the Editors

The Texas Association of Creative Writing Teachers' annual gathering provides a serious but welcoming venue for members of the organization to share their pedagogical and creative work in a series of panels over several days. This inaugural issue of *Writing Texas* offers selections of the best poetry, prose, and pedagogy presented at the TACWT meeting in September 2013. Out of the enthusiasm and camaraderie of this meeting arose the idea for *Writing Texas*. Dr. Jerry Craven, Press Director for Lamar University Press, generously offered to publish this collection for the organization and provided the stunning cover photograph. I am most grateful to Dr. Craven for his vast experience as a writer and publisher and for his consistently good humor in bringing this first-ever TACWT collection to fruition. I appreciate the executive group's confidence in giving me the opportunity to co-edit this first volume of *Writing Texas* and Marilyn Robitaille for sharing that opportunity with me.

—Julie Chappell

If you're published somewhere—okay anywhere—you know that feeling when you see your name in print. It's manifest with a little squint of the eyes, an extra palpitation of the heart, a distinctive taste of something sweet in your mouth. Seeing our names in print confirms us. It lets us know that we *are*, that we exist, and that somewhere in deep space we will be remembered. This volume is a celebration and a testimony of the desire to be read, of what it means to share. To know that our efforts to cross time and space, circumstance and detail, to reach out to anyone who will take the time to read us is a big, good thing. Here, we are comrades and conspirators in our desire to chase the muses. On the page we are made entirely out of language; in the flesh we commune at an annual meeting. And that's the wonder of this volume of literature. What you are about to read in *Writing Texas* in uniquely the product of the Texas Association of Creative Writing Teachers. A group of people who study the craft, who participate in the communal substance, and who, above all, desire to share the magic. I am honored to co-edit this first volume of *Writing Texas*; it exists because of the talent of the TACWT membership, the tireless efforts of co-editor Julie Chappell, and the stunning talents of Jerry Craven. Enjoy.

—Marilyn Robitaille

CONTENTS

Poetry and Prose

TACWT 2013 Student Award Winners

Pedagogical Approaches

Poetry and Prose

Pennie Boyett

My Archer City

If every writer needs an Archer City,
       How do I find mine?
Where is the map?

In this desolate landscape, this movie set of a town,
       what I need to push against
       while discovering my story?

This place works for McMurtry.
He resists its claim when he is here,
And then, when he removes himself,
       he paints it with words so knowing, so true,
       as a parent loves an imperfect child,

That a world of readers recognizes it as home,
And the town, stripped bare in this knowing, pushes back.
Where is my Archer City?
What must I resist in a mighty effort,
       in order to write the story of my life?

Charlotte Renk

Witness(II)

And a God of unknown origin and ragged persuasion
swept upon Nina again, convicting her mission
with a presence more menacing than stringent
smoke following her, more terrifying than the
Aye-aye crouching on the edge of darkness, waiting
till the circle where she stooped and stared
into the fire flickered and smoldered into ash.

She knows the hungry eyes of the Aye-aye
determined toward the blackening blaze;
she hears the terrible ears twitch beyond
his rat face, and she accepts the Way
of long-pointed claws and sharp incisors.

Smoke and stench drench her will. She's tired.
Now, violet hope, like madras, bleeds to gray
after too many washes. She'd failed to stop
anything: beatings of Brother after he'd wet
and wept and prayed, the rape of a sister, leaned
yellow dressed, open-legged against the bus;
to stop that even after Bergen-Belsen. *Cleansing*
slaughters swept Poland, Bosnia, Darfur,
and oh...oh so much and no more!

She was no bodhisattva dripping ambrosia to hell;
no Dalai Lama laughing, calling on kindness still.
Why hadn't she or the blessed Aye-aye already
gnawed the claws from Karadzic and her father?
Judgment rages now in the claw of a rat sniffing,
twitching, scratching in the bracken.

Nina's heart weighs a thousand, thousand pounds
of leaden nothing against a swallow's feather,
laid upon the scale. And the Aye-aye waits.
Should she, like Jesus, who called for song

and dance after his Last Supper, rise and jig
before Golgotha, before the little Aye-aye
takes communion.

This Fifth Season...II

of the *Heavenly Pivot* begs reflection.
And today, I drape the shawl of *why*
across my shoulders, bent by all
that's wrong.

I long to "fix" those who suffer
poverty and brokenness,
but my long silence shreds this shawl,
and I sit frozen between tempest and peace,
between will and surrender

for women the world over who weep
for their hungry ones or their young sons
who risk raised fists against injustice.

For children betrayed by grown un-adults
whose brokenness robbed innocence.

For those who need safe food,
thirst for clean water, gasp for fresh air
from a land, ravaged by greed,
plagued by waste.

And for my daughter, little twig
who sought art's light, arced air, dazzled sun
...till disappointment, distrust snuffed her light,
snapped the twig.

I could not say the sad I saw, I see.

As if Culture's Dr. depressed my tongue
stabbing palate stick so far down my throat,
I could only gag and "aaawgh," stomach lurching
to heave such truths.

Too silent, too long, my tongue sparks
now like a dry wick flickering...,

No...more like a stricken drought-parched pine
igniting to set the whole wood on fire.

I am both wick and wood!
Too silent too long, We reap what I have sown—
sad silence in this room.

And as I finger space between worn threads
of this old shawl I wear, I swear earthly pivot here:

I'll shed this ragged wrap of silent *why's;*
hushed silence shrieks in darkened rooms.
I'll pull each frayed and sagging thread,
then stitch loves voice to awful truths .

Human Wood

May I enter Care's fire for *you*
    my dear friend,
    my child,
    my love,
    my poem,
so willing to be consumed,
knowing I will be consumed,
knowing that this dry-wood log of self
must enter the fire, that I
    disappear into its light,
    radiate its warmth,
    rise in its smoke,
    flicker its last embers
till I lie light as a ragged mound of ash
ready to scatter by wind.

May *you* know, Friend, Child, Love, Poem that
    that's *why* I am here,
    that's *how* I can *stand* to be here,
    and that's the only *way*
I can ever let you go.

Dan Williams

Gog and Magog

Gog and Magog have no jobs. Monstrous twins
abandoned behind Wal-Mart, they collect Welfare
and sell a little crystal meth on weekends
 at the bowling alley. No longer interested in
the butchery of innocents, they only pillage
Albertson's for chips, Oreos, salted nuts, and Little
Debbies. They sleep till noon in beds equally fetid,
in a cheap condo filled with filth, Goodwill
furniture, and a wicked sixty-inch plasma TV. They
prefer reality-TV shows of hapless fools
and mean-spirited deceivers, but they are fond
 of Jeopardy, the Wheel of Fortune, and the original
Star Trek series. They sit for hours in the dark,
their front room lit only by the flickering images of
Alex Trebett, Vanna White, and Captain Kirk.

Yet every afternoon, relentlessly,
they climb the big hill to watch the bloody
eternal spectacle of the giant eagle tear
out and devour Prometheus's liver,
never growing the slightest bit tired
of gore and agony, the butchery
sanctioned by wrathful gods. Gog and Magog
are endlessly fascinated by the monstrous
bird's capacity to shred flesh with its
razor-like talons and beak and pluck out
the blood-blackened organ. Silently they
watch, grimly satisfied with the endless
show Olympian vengeance for paltry
 theft. They like the way Prometheus howls
in pain and yanks his chains, the way the bird
tosses pieces of liver to itself
in the air, snapping at them with its bloody
beak, and the way both Titan and bird seem
to sigh afterwards, both a bit awkward,

embarrassed, and shy. After the bird flaps
its heavy wings, rising slowly in the air,
and after Prometheus turns away to
spend another day waiting on his rock,
Gog and Magog light Salems and trudge slowly
back down to their squalid condo hoping
to catch another episode of *Survivor*.

My Other Self

Past purgatory, far below hell, there's an
Antipoedean world of otherwise,
A continent of contrary where other
Sides denounce conventions and delight in
Substandardizations; there my other self
Cavorts with legions of fallen angels
disreputable minor gods, and mythic
beasts no longer fashionable, a friend to
griffons, centaurs, gorgons, harpies, and all
furies; he carries an irritable
 basilisk named Nicodemos in his coat
pocket, both self and lizard smoke Salems;
unrequited, he pursues a maenad
named Peaches, whose colorful history
has been immortalized on the walls of ten
thousand truck stops; she takes his cigarettes
and money but prefers intimate contact
 with a tattooed felon named Big Boy. My self
otherwise spends his endless days writing
wretched lyrics for a rock band named Gestalt,
who ridicule him for clichés, but send
him out to score crack, meth, and strawberry
licorice; my other self is peevish,
 boorish, dull, and insecure; he eats too
much fat and grows fat, and he neglects to
bathe, brush his teeth, or change his underwear.
The lesser gods of forgotten faiths and
Two-bit actors of old B-movies all
Laugh at him, and even Nicodemos
Tires of his company and would gladly

Abandon him for a better host, but
For the Salems. Yet my other self remains
Oblivious, resolute, and stoic;
Late afternoons he sits on a rock quietly
Drinking cheap rum in warm diet Pepsi,
Watching the molten sky, not wondering if,
why, and what for, but where he might that night
find Peaches, and even Nicodemos,
hissing on his knee, finds a measure of peace.

Poor Apostrophe

The apostrophe took sick,
lingered, then died delusional,
imagining life eternal, a feverish
restless dream, killed by a viral
infection, an ineluctable contagion.
Doctors despaired, prescribed
large lime tablets, sulfuric poultices,
plasters, and liniments to no avail,
finally resorting to steroid injections
and IV drips of precious fluids.
They lectured, consulted, raved,
and ranted while the patient
declined. Mourners gathered,
an aged lot, lamenting the loss,
one or two caressed crosses,
muttering about possession,
resurrection, and canonization,
and some less sanctimonious
intoned, a good life, a full life.

Dave Parsons

Color of Mourning

She awakened to Texas summer bright
in her eyes, throwing on a new yellow
robe, she dragged her body into the kitchen
to make coffee which she dug from a deep
yellow decanter. Awareness steeps through
the heart beating perks, her eyes fall on the child's
drawing that was stuck on the refrigerator door,
a yellow duck swimming on deep dark
water under another bloody sun brimming
with amber iris—Iris, goddess of the rainbow,
adding to the litany of golden messengers, all
bringing to her mind the dress, the yellow
dress that she had given to her niece
for her fifth birthday, the sweet lemon
yellow dress that the child delighted in so
that today she was to be buried in it—the sanctuary
of the summer kitchen felt unusually cold
as she cracked a single egg, spilling
carefully the delicate yoke onto melting butter
thinking, yellow—yellow—
yellow should not feel like this.

First published in *Louisiana Literature*, Fall/Winter, 2003; *Color of Mourning*, Texas Review Press/Texas A&M University Press Consortium, 2007

Keys

There is a certain amount of amazement, when
you have been typing for a while
and you glance up, finding
that you have been writing
in some foreign untold language, coming
with the greatest of ease, hands
flying through the wrong keys
of the keyboard.

This seems to be the way
that much of my life has gone—every
now and again finding
that I have been living with great confidence
a life based on false premises.

Snapping In

> *And already/nothing remains of the warrior but his*
> *weapons/and his gaze.*
>   —Ted Hughes, *The Knight.*

That is what my Drill Instructors called it, snapping
in, lying in the prone position for an untold time,

learning the nuances of integrating body and weapon,
arm tightly wrapped, trapped within the riffle sling's

noose, legs spread, elbows flexed into a natural tripod,
eyes searing through the narrow vortex of the battle

sights of an M-1A-1 gas operated, air cooled, semi-
automatic shoulder weapon, squeezing the trigger,

over and over and over and again, wishing for live rounds
to fire, hearing only the crisp jolting snaps of the firing pin

wondering, wandering through the dull soundless voids
of time and thought, occasionally finding melodic notes

of a kind of muscle memory, not unlike years later, standing
in the brisk cold waters of the Snake River, casting over

and over, and over into herds of galloping torrents, white
manes chaotically stampeding mountain stones and Rainbows

and there—and there—and there, something wild, thrashing,
leaping ahead to a murky watery future, returning back, again

having no idea of the time that passes; when attempting
to move, numb, dumb legs, boots finding only slimy smooth

feral stones on the muted face of the yellowish green river
bottom, for an instant, the same hooked heart of the trout

in me flying from one element of air to another, and falling
rock hard, sniped, splayed body instantly awash in the icy, jolting

revelations that must eventually come to the minds of most all
falling bodies, that last flashing white epiphany—and then only

the sounding, drumming eternal waters, the steely tugging tow
of a destined time that must come to us all, of being snapped up—

First published in TCU Press/Texas A&M University Press Consortium, 2012

Janet McCann

Answering Machine

I call my house, it's empty
and my own voice responds,
painfully hesitant, saying I'm
unavailable. I can hear
gaps in the apology, the whirring
tape, a stammer, a repetition,
an indrawn breath, then finally
and blessedly, the beep.

And I had redone that three times,
the first inaudible, the second
grammatically incorrect, and then
this one. I listen to the tape
recording silence, an expectant
hum, and I hang up.

If it was all that hard
just to express absence,
then how can I begin
to tell you that I'm here?

T-Shirt

says he was there, at the Cotton Bowl,
the Jubilee Celebration, the Fiftieth Anniversary
of the Pine Creek Baptist Church.

says that Christ is the light,
that Molson is beautiful and good, that a baby
grows beneath the arrow, that Salvador Dali

is just now munching his morning bowl of surreal.
That she is a member of the NRA,
that his team won in the Cotton Bowl.

Body bumper-stickers on the time
of your life, hunched haunches in
jeans, I don't get mad I get

even, International Screwing Team,
Christ with a foaming chalice, This Blood's For
You, piety or blasphemy? All of them

wanting to be read, but not looked at,
to be seen, but look at your own risk and only sideways
and if you can read this, you're too damn close.

Life List
in memory of S.A.

My friend the scholar-birdwatcher
is dying, after a quiet regular life
of Milton and birds, and if I could

imagine him a farewell, it would be this:
to look out into the small yard
he tended for forty years, to where

he placed the bird houses, the martin
house and the hummingbird feeder,
just in time to see a sweep of air

curve in and take form, the great arctic gyrfalcon
not on his life list, there on the sill,
to be recognized by beak, feathers and pinions

and final knowledge, Adam's homecoming
after the story's end, better than Eden.
May he have in his hand a feather, that his wife

might know where he has gone.

Jerry Bradley

Evil Twins

long ago and far away
are a fairy tale, a couple
like dog and pony –
duplicate offspring
of debauched trolls

but if all brothers are grim
then one day may marry
another and still another
until the whole year seduces
and something misbegotten
whispers like a suicide
in the daily news

the risk is needless

when a star dies
a farmer may dream a hundred suns
to make his glum garden green

and what grows grows on credit
always borrowing
against someone else's bank

if one crop fails
something curious
nonetheless grows

until a night in a hotel
and one under a bridge
become similar perils

and what flies from the window
could be pigeons
or just old love letters
breaking in every direction

Lonesome

When George Gobel told the Rat Pack he felt
like a pair of brown shoes, we understood.
"Well then there now," he said
as if anticipating the failed surgery ahead.

Hank Sr. knew the moan of whippoorwills and trains
and nearly wept, and Dylan's maid
bore a large family yet died a friendless death,
done in by a casually-tossed cane.

Patchen said our lives were meaningless
because the years were cruel;
then he fell off an OR table,
another paralyzed fool

until he too found his remedy among the dead.
And it echoes among us at every turn:
on the trail of the pine, in Bill Monroe's Kentuckiana sound
and McCarthy's apocalyptic border town,

when Elvis wonders if we are tonight.
In time even the unhurried tortoise
reaches the end of the line.
Slowed by the entropy of words, we know

that what we say is seldom what we mean
(even when uttered to the slenderest soul).
Call it our unpaid debt to the Phoenecians
for letters and the Maya (of course)
who in their misery first understood the need for o.

The Woman Who Disliked Kissing

beneath a tree of splendid yellows
the season turns in an outdoor café
a menu of crabs and scallops
a caravel in casual heaps

14

informal, harvested for sentiment
and ceremony, an evening of plum flowers
on a mirrored muraled wall

but these surfaces mean nothing
no matter how much moonlight
spills onto her heart

she is just canvas, something plain
upon which the night
repeatedly misspeaks itself
its pasty telegrams rumble through her
like a freight with many cars

she stores sadness in her pulse
is disappointed by the sweetness
that descends
                          and fearful that the autumn
interruptive and breakable as the slightest oath
has always been more secure, more trusting
than her soft uncommittable kiss

Jim Sanderson

Bankers

I got a fair amount of money and a certain degree of respect among my business associates. I consider myself a salesman. I provide things for people. Which is different from a banker. But long time ago, I could have become a banker.

Here is how it was. I am just graduated high school and have no clue about what I'm going to do with my life. College seems like some foreign country, so I take the tests but only apply at San Antonio Junior College. My mother and several friends told me to go to college and study enough to make Ds so as to stay out of the war with a college deferment. My father said he fought for his country and so his son should fight for his country sos I should just wait to be drafted. I didn't know if he meant it was just *his* country or I had a part of it too.

Most of my friends from the Southside had working people like my parents, so they just didn't know what to do. Of course, I had schoolmates who enlisted, who went off to some college land, or who smoked a lot of pot and became hippies. So I figured just to go back to work for the downtown bank I had worked at the summer before—and wait to decide or see what happened.

My father said I should be careful of that bank. He showed me the headlines. Steves Bank, started by one of San Antonio's old, rich German families, got bought out by Sammy White, this south Texas rancher and businessman who was being sued by half the state. Sammy White had a habit, my father said, of turning things to shit while he came out smelling like a rose.

But I went back to work for the Steves Bank anyway. At first, because I liked downtown, especially in the summer mornings when the stores would send their cleaning crews to hose off the sidewalks, outside tables and chairs. They'd wash away the spilled beer, piss, puke, or whatever was on those sidewalks and get ready for another pounding from a hot afternoon. Downtown mornings, for me, was the smell of hose water on warming concrete and little rainbow arches filtering through the spray. It was all fresh and new and clean in the morning, making me think my life would just work out. So I'd catch the second earliest express bus to downtown and walk around right up until bank opening time. I'd even walk through alleys, through the sterno cans, wine bottles, and pigeon bones, waking up the bums, and thinking, who knows, but what I might end up eating pigeons in a downtown alley. Typical of me back then, I'd figure that being a bum might even have its plus side.

So in I walk for my first day, back to my little cubbyhole where I help the head teller, and there to greet me is Emmitt. Emmitt is this old guy nearly eighty who retired as a bank vice president years before and then when his wife died, went back to work at a bank. Banking is just what he does. He dresses banking style. He wears a coat and tie, but when he takes off his coat he has these old sleeve garters pushed up to his elbows. And when he is stooped over counting for a long time, he wears one of those tinted eye shades. Emmett's eyes are sunk deep in his head with dark circles all around them. He's got hair growing out his ears and nose, and his eyebrows are twisted into points like the old time moustaches, but his head is slick, shiny bald with some rough, brown splotches on it. When he sees me, his old eyes get watery, and this old man hugs me.

Then I notice on the top of his slick old head is the shape of a perfect pair of red lips. I wipe at it with my fingers. "What's this?" I ask.

Then Becky, prettiest of the tellers, looks over and says, "I got to kiss my boyfriends."

Doris, the head teller, gives me my orders, which are the same every day. While dumpy Doris, with her curled-toe, elf slippers, sucks on her cigarettes and peers out the window of her office to watch the younger, prettier tellers—some of who tease me about being young and manly and able, I grab the bagged coins collected the day before and dump them into the coin rolling machine and watch it as it sputters and tries to spit out rolls of quarters, nickels, dimes, or pennies. Sometimes it just chokes, and the coins and the paper rolls gush out of the chute. So then I sweep and scoop up all the spilled coins and dump them back in the machine while Doris frowns at me and the machine.

After spilling coins in the morning, I'd work with Emmitt in the afternoons, and he'd train me to be a teller. The year before, with his garter sleeves and visor on, he taught me how to grab a stack of bills, bend back a corner, and flip through them by fives with my thumb. He could count money faster than anybody in the bank, faster than the machine that could only count crisp, new bills, and after he closed out at the end of the day, he'd help out all the pretty teller girls. When I first worked with him, we had run out of calculator paper and I was changing it, and he yelled, "Don't throw away that roll." I held up the empty cardboard paper roll, and he nodded and said "When the circus comes to town, they buy those to make assholes for hobby horses." He'd smile when he said a joke like that; then he'd just go back to counting money. And the tellers would giggle and sometimes kiss him on the forehead.

And the summer before was Hemisfair year, so all sorts of freaks and crooks would come in. So these two short change artists come in. They were dressed flashy in colors so bright you had to squint at them. So while one guy was scooting around the bank, the other guy comes up to Emmitt and asks for change for a hundred in twenties and tens and fives. Emmitt motions me over, and I watch as the guy then asks for change for a twenty, then for a fifty, and Emmitt interrupts him and asks if he didn't want a different bill. Turns out Emmitt gyped the short change guy and kept him there long enough for a downtown beat cop to escort him out. Then there was the time Emmitt calls me over and tells me to stare long and hard at two twenties he was counting. When I held them up the light, I could see short thin red and blue veins, but they looked drawn. And so they were. So Emmitt lets me call the F.B.I. and give them the report, and the F.B.I. and some guys from the Secret Service and the Federal Reserve come look at the bills and thank me for my sharp eyes.

So on my first day back, after rolling coins, I'm at lunch, eating a sandwich in our little lunch room and looking at the sizzling concrete outside, and Emmitt comes up to me. He has his carrots and celery all cut in nice pieces just about all the same length, and he has his tuna fish on white bread with the crust cut off. He was classy like that. "So, Gregory," always "Gregory," he says, not "Greg," "are you considering your future?" Whenever somebody older said *future*, I always figured I was getting a lecture.

"I'm mostly waiting on my future to find me," I say.

Emmitt smiles, "You know, anymore, a banker needs a degree."

"So you think I could be a banker?"

"I'm not just talking about being a teller, now Gregory, but I'm talking about being a loan officer, a Vice President even."

"So you think that I could do that."

"I don't know. You have to study. You have keep up with the banking world."

"I could do that."

"Yes, I think you can. But you should want to. People forget that bankers help people. Bankers make things possible for people." He waits to see if I'm thinking or not. "You ought to go to college, then

18

become a banker."

I start nodding my head and munching from my sandwich while Emmitt takes a dainty bite out of his tuna fish, "But now," Emmitt leans closer and lowers his voice. "Be careful of *this* bank."

I lean across the lunch room table and my forehead nearly touches Emmitt's. "What's wrong with this bank?"

"The new owner. He doesn't appreciate banking."

Emmitt leans away from me and frowns while he chews his sandwich. From the lines in his forehead and the way his eyes seemed to sink back further into his forehead, I can see that Sammy White scares poor ol' Emmitt.

So, I close out the day with Emmitt. Emmitt and me go into the main vault, and we look at the bagged money and we count it. With Emmitt looking over my shoulder and smiling because I got faster from the last summer, I count the bags of old bills that we have stashed and will soon be sending over to the Federal Reserve building to be burned.

Since then, I've thought a lot about the life of that money and the use it served and the way it must have helped people—and maybe even hurt them—and then of it all just going up in smoke and out the chimney above the Reserve. And back then, with that money in front of me is when I actually started thinking I would like to be a banker.

And Emmitt must have been thinking too because, when I turn around from counting the money in record time, and this my first day, he is smiling at me. "Well, my, my, you just tugged right on through that little chore," Emmitt says to me. Emmitt nods serious-like, but then a little light flickered inside Emmitt's scarred, bald head, and he starts smiling again, "Gregory, do you play tennis?"

"I've tried."

"Would you like to try this Saturday?" Emmitt asks me, and I say "Sure."

And after work, with the heat bouncing off the sidewalks and boiling me, I walk a little around downtown, by the old public library with its cement lion and elephant out front and sit on the steps in the shade. I get just a little cooler. Over to my left, down the street, next to the river is the site of the new glass library building. And soon, they will move all the books out of this building, and the cement lion and elephant won't have the people gawking at them and the kids pretending to ride them. And to my right in the distance, looking over the simmering city is the Tower of America, built for Hemisfair. And two years before, it was just a pole sticking into the sky. And I start to think about my future. The war comes sneaking back up on me as well as the idea of college.

And for while there, that day, I thought that Emmitt's idea about what a banker was was what I should be.

* * *

So, that Saturday, at noon, I drive the clunker that my father bought for me, a '61 Plymouth Valiant with a pushbutton transmission under the dash, to San Pedro Park tennis courts. Emmitt is there waiting for me in his tennis outfit. He has shorts down to about his knees, and his legs bow out from those white shorts. He has on a white tennis shirt with an orange stripe on the collar and down the short sleeves. He's got a bucket-like tennis hat squshed on his head. He has a racket under one arm, another racket in his hand, and a cooler in his other hand. "You want to warm up?" Emmitt says to me.

So I jog to the far side of a court, and I peek over my shoulder at Emmitt hobbling up behind me, old man style. It's like he needs both those bowed legs under him at the same time, so he won't tip over. So I figure that I can beat the hell out of this guy taking those choppy steps. I get to the far side of the court, watch, and jump in place, noticing that sweat has already started to run down my forehead into my eyes and that the sun seems to be pressing on the top of my head. Emmitt sets the cooler down near the tall fence and then quick steps to the court. He still has both rackets—one in his hand and one under his arm. He bends over, then makes his body just sort of shake, like a wet dog. Then he pulls a tennis ball out of his pocket, bounces it, and hits it to me.

I watch the ball and try to give it a hard whack back over the net. And then I notice, Emmitt is playing with a racket in each hand. He lobs the ball into one corner of the court, and I have to run to get to it. I whack it hard again, just over the net. Emmitt shuffles to the ball and just gets a racket under it to lob it again—to the far corner of court. And I run to get it. The old fart is ambidextrous. He runs slower than a girl, but I can get nothing past him because he's got nearly six feet of range with those two rackets. And all he does is lob, and I run. I beat him for the point. Then I beat him the first game. But my knees feel weak. And my eyes are blurred and burning with sweat in them. So I ask for a drink. I get a drink, Emmitt doesn't.

So this old man baby-stepping up and back, right and left around the court, lobbing nearly every shot, me taking long tugs at the water after every game, just wears my ass out. He beats me 6-3, for set, and asks if I want to play another one. I am so tired I can't even talk, but Emmitt glances up at the sun and says, "We better not push it. Sunstroke weather." I smile and try to jog to him, but I can barely make my feet work. After I take a drink, he upends the water over his head and smiles at me while he drips. And when he leaves, he climbs into his twelve-year-old Rambler and waves real rapid-like to me as he pulls out of the tennis courts' parking lot.

I had to think about Emmitt that whole weekend. I mean, I thought he was attached to the bank. I couldn't imagine him outside of the little teller's booth he was in. And here he is kicking kids' assess in tennis and, from remembering his little grin, I couldn't help but think he was kinda proud of the ass kicking.

* * *

By the time I get back to work on Monday, I'm actually thinking better and better of Emmitt. When I dare to, I turn my back to the coin rolling machine and go out and stare at him and catch him napping a time or two. And I'm thinking even harder about college and some degree and then a life as a banker—counting old money, catching short-change artists, finding counterfeit money, helping people—when I hear a scream, and then Doris yelling at me to run downstairs.

I zap out the Head Teller's office and then out the door of the filing room, into the upstairs lobby, and then I run down the down escalator, three steps at a time, until I'm in front of the automatic door next to the street, and I'm looking at this whimpering, pregnant Mexican girl, sprawled out on the floor inside the bank. And to one side of her is square-faced, Brylcreemed Hank Worley, one of Steves' vice presidents, and to the other side of her is a man in a LBJ hat, string tie, blue-striped seersucker suit, pointy-toed boots, and a wet umbrella. I think to look up and see there is a sheet of rain outside, and I see what has happened. Somebody forgot to put the rubber mat inside the door, and this poor girl steps in from out of the rain, slips on the hard, slick tiles, and cracks her ass on the floor. The LBJ cowboy and Hank exchange looks, and then the woman screams: "Sue."

Not really thinking, I step forward, slip a little myself, and try to help the lady up. When I grab her arm and she tries to let me pull her up, she blurts out in pain as she tries to put her foot down. "Shit," I hear Hank say.

I kind of half drag and half carry her to the carpet and let her lie down, and I hear, "Who is this boy?"

"This is Gregory Newman," Hank Worley says. "He works here summers."

The girl snivels and says, "Sue."

"Well, he seems to know how to handle hisself," the LBJ cowboy says. And I see some keys dangling in front of me. "Mr. Gregory, can you drive?"

"Yes sir," I say.

"Those keys are to my wife's Cadillac. It's parked in the garage in my space. You pull it out front. Treat her real nice, but get her into the back seat all comfortable, and then get her to the emergency room at Santa Rosa. And then you stay with her and make sure she's happy."

"What's your space?" I ask. Hank Worley breathes in.

"It's the big one, right next to the door," the man says.

"This is Mr. White," Hank says.

Mr. White says, "I'm the fella owns about sixty-percent of this place."

"Sue," the woman says.

"Will do," I say, grab the keys, and turn around. Up at the second floor, looking down at me and nodding his head, like he just woke up from his nap, is ol' Emmitt.

I run out the backdoor of the bank, take a right, and duck into the underground parking lot, and sure enough, sitting in its place with a sign saying *Mr. White* is Sammy White's wife's lime green Cadillac with a white vinyl top. I open the door and slide in on the white leather seat. Before I start it up, I just rub on that seat to get the slick, oiled feel of the leather. Then I start it up, and I turn on the air. I find the knob for the radio and click in on and turn the dial to hear and feel the throb from the back speakers.

By the time I get to the front of the bank and barely remember to turn off the radio, Hank and Mr. Sammy White have the crying lady by the arms and are guiding her toward the curb. People stop and stare. Hank opens the back seat passenger door as smiling Sammy White guides her in, then gently pushes her across the backseat so that she is laying across it. I shiver when she muffles a scream, and I look at Hank's face in the open passenger side door, and his face tells me I better not fuck up.

As I'm trying to remember which downtown streets go which way and around what to get to Santa Rosa, the lady in back sniffles. I glance in the rearview mirror and see tears on her face. With my left hand on the wheel, I reach behind the front seat with my right, and she grabs my hand and squeezes it. And then she says, again, "Sue."

So I eventually pull into the Emergency room, open the backdoor, and help the limping lady into the hospital. It is mid morning, but already, bleeding and otherwise hurt people are crowding in. I reach for her purse, and first she tugs it away from me, but then lets me have it. I find a wallet and a fake looking social security card and a driver's license. She screams. Then I start screaming. And soon, I have nurses around me, and I'm trying to explain that the woman is hurt, and they explain that the woman has no insurance, and I yell louder. They say that they need to contact the next of kin. Then I yell that I am the next of kin. When they look at me, something takes possession of me, and I say, "That's right. What you looking at? I'm her husband."

"What's your wife's name?"

"Maria Newman."

"How you going to pay for this visit?"

"Do we look like we can pay for this?"

So I suddenly have a lot of forms in front of me, and I am writing down *Maria Newman* and wishing I could have thought faster and come up with some other name. And then they get that pregnant lady into a wheel chair, and I hold her hand, and she cries, and she motions I should bend over her so she can tell me something. And with her hot breath on my ear, she says a number. "Su Esposo?" I ask. She nods, and then, I phone her husband.

Emilio isn't too good with English either, but he is better than her. And he makes me to understand that he will be at the hospital as soon as he can. So then I call Hank Worley, and he says to stay there until I am sure how she is. And then he says, "You see if this 'sue' idea stays in her head."

"What about Mr. White's car?"

"I've already talked to him about that. You drive the car back to the bank when you get through." But Hank Worley keeps breathing into the phone, like he isn't through talking to me yet "Now you be careful with that car," he says.

So I wait and wait. I'm drinking cokes and eating chips and peanut butter crackers from the vending machine. Finally, they wheel that lady back and tell me—her husband—that she has a sprained ankle and knee and that our baby is fine. A nurse says she is more scared than anything, so they pumped her up with some sedatives. She smiles at me and, she reaches up from her wheel chair and takes my hand again. The nurse tells me that my wife is dismissed.

I wheel her out of the hospital, and then I have to give the wheelchair back, so she stands up and puts the new crutches under her arm. We walk to a bench under a cottonwood, sit in the still damp air, and wait for Emilio. Her name is Tristina. And she tells me she will not sue. And when Emilio shows up, she hugs him, and he picks her up off the ground, and I follow behind them carrying her crutches as Emilio carries her to his pick up and stuffs her in the cab, and I throw the crutches in the back. The last I see of that pretty, scared lady, she has her head swiveled around to look out the back windshield of the truck to see me waving goodbye.

Now, still, I think about that woman once in awhile. Mostly, she wasn't hurt, but she was scared. English was new to her, probably the city was new too, and she was just about to panic. And I can look back and figure that this was where Emmitt's notion of banking comes in. I was helping her. I was kind of a banker. But when I think that, I remember that the word the coming out her mouth was "sue. Everybody is always selling something.

So, by the time I get back to the bank, it is closed. I pull Sammy White's Cadillac up to the backside of the building right next to the parking garage. And there, sitting on the bench the tellers put out so they could have lunch outside on nice days is Mr. Sammy White, pretty as you please, eating an orange. He has his seersucker suit coat folded up and sitting behind him, and he has his LBJ hat pulled low over his eyes. I get out the Cadillac and inch toward Mr. White. "Have a sit," he says.

I sit beside Mr. White. He looks out at the steam from rain rising off the asphalt and cement and cuts a slice out of his orange with his pocket knife. He spears that slice of orange with his pocket knife blade and pokes it toward me. "Orange slice?" he asks. I thank him and take the slice of orange. "You know, one of the reasons I bought this bank is I like the smell of water from a hose splashing on cement, the kind of way it splashes up and makes everything feel cleaner."

"I know just exactly what you mean," I say. He pokes another slice at me. I pull it from the knife, bite into it, and feel the spray of orange juice inside my mouth.

"But this evaporating rain makes it all steamy. It's nasty."

"I would have got you your car back, but Mr. Worley told me to wait, and they just couldn't get that woman fixed."

"So did she say anymore about suing?"

"She's not going to sue."

"How do you know?"

"She was just scared."

"You sure?"

"She told me she wasn't."

"You believe her?"

"Yes."

Sammy White slides another slice of orange to me and pops the last slice into his mouth. "Then I'd say you done a fair day's work."

"Sorry, I didn't get your car back."

"You like that car?"

"That's a nice car, sir."

"Good job, Gregory." He stands up, walks to the car, and looks over it. "Toss me the keys." I toss him the keys. He opens up the door, throws his suit coat in, then he throws his LBJ hat in and turns to me. "I'll see you at work, Gregory. I might have another job for you."

* * *

So the next day, Doris slips into her curly-toed Elf shoes, sucks on her cigarette, and shakes her head as she listens to me. Emmitt, who gets his run of the whole teller area in back of the counter—even Doris's office—listens and rubs his flat palm over his shiny but patchy bald head. "That should never have happened," Doris says.

"Looks like you might have saved the bank some money," Emmitt says. "You did well."

I puff out for Emmitt, but then he adds, "But now you be careful of that Sammy White."

"He seems like an alright guy to me," I say.

"You be careful," he says, and I go back to rolling my coins.

But then mid-week comes, and with Doris gawking, I get a call on Doris' phone. Now let me repeat that, I get a call. I am nobody and somebody is calling on Doris' phone. And Doris' face scrunches all up and then just drops, showing wrinkles I had never seen before. And she slowly lowers the phone from her ear and says, "Mr. White wants to see you."

I can feel Emmitt's eyes staring at my back as I round Doris' office door. And waiting by the executive office is square-faced, slick-haired Hank Worley telling me just with his eyes not to fuck up. And then Hank Worley opens the door—for me.

In I step. And there behind his mahogany desk, under one of those blue-bonnet and wagon wheel pictures, is Sammy White cracking pecans with his hands. He puts two nuts together, then squeezes them between his clasped palms, and I hear a crack. Then he pulls the cracked nut apart and digs at the meat with his pocket knife. "People do good for me, I like to do good by them."

"Thank you sir," I say and notice that there's this chair in front of him, but he doesn't ask me to sit, just stares at those pecans.

"You like that Cadillac?"

"Oh yes, sir."

"How'd you like to go on a little road trip?"

"Fine sir."

"How you like to take a brand new, just bought Cadillac on that road trip?"

"Sir?"

"Reason I had my wife's Cadillac was I was shopping for her a new one. And I found one. So I want you to drive that new Cadillac down to my ranch the other side of Freer, pick up my Cadillac, and drive it back."

He looks intently at his pecan, opens his palms to look at his reward, gouges out some pecan meat, chews, and then smiles at me. "And here's some pecans for you." And Sammy White, the man himself, gets up from his desk and rounds its corner and hands me a sack of pecans and the keys to his wife's new Cadillac. "You can eat them nuts on the way down. Best get started. It's a drive to get there in back in one day."

* * *

Mrs. Sammy White's new Cadillac is a kind of a Maroon with another white leather interior. The radio is top quality and nearly shatters the windows. And in the glove compartment is Mrs. White's 8-track collection, mostly country western and some soft, syrupy stuff by Andy Williams. But I make my way through most all of her tapes as I cruise through the cactus fields and staring cattle, eating my boss's pecans—then on to Freer and past and then down a paved country road to a double-wide gate over a cattle guard with *White Ranch* written on an arch stretching over the gate. Then I drive another mile on—get this—on a paved road, up to the long, low, new ranch house.

I pull up in front, walk up the curving stone sidewalk, and knock on the door. A woman with several strands of hair hanging in her face and some smeared mascara answers the door. Then I see more. She has on a bikini top with cleavage trying to push that top off, a pair of Wrangler jeans, and boots. In her hand is one of those fancy drink glasses with the long stem up under a bowl, and what I guess is a margarita or martini is splashing out the sides of that glass. "Mrs. White?" I ask.

The woman steps past me to look out across the front yard to the Cadillac parked at the end of the sidewalk. "That's mine, I'm guessing," she says and sways in front of me. And I'm noticing for an older woman she has her butt packed into her Wranglers as nice as she has her chest packed into that bikini top.

"Brand new Cadillac," I say. And she turns around and walks right past me, and without turning around says, "Name is Cheryl. You want a drink."

"No, I don't think I want a drink. In fact, I better get back because it's a long drive, and I don't have much daylight, and I'm on the clock so to speak . . .

"Come in," Cheryl White says, and I know that it is an order, and she is my boss's wife, so I follow her in, and she shuts the door after me. I keep walking, figuring I'm in a living room, but it's so damn big I walk and walk and can't figure out where I'm going. I pass a sofa and come up to another one, and then I get my order, "Stop."

Mrs. White pours me whatever she is having into a glass like hers, and carrying my glass and hers in one hand and the pitcher in the other, sloshing liquor out of the glasses and the pitcher, she steps toward me all slinky-like and hands me the glass "Sit," she orders. I sit on the sofa. "Can I take that pitcher from you?" I ask. She hands it to me with one hand, and I take it and realize that this woman must have some hell of some muscles from hauling that pitcher of liquor around the house with her, and I sit in on a lamp table with both hands. She hands me my drink, and I sip it. It is gin, nearly straight, and I start to cough.

"So what do you think is going on here?" Mrs. White asks me.

I take another sip of the gin, which to me tastes like carrot juice, and I say "I mean, well I don't know, you mean with me and you having a drink?"

"I mean with fucking everything." She takes her wet napkin from her drink and wipes at her chest just above her cleavage. I take another sip of the carrot juice

"You're the wife of the boss."

"Right. So why do you think you drove my yearly gift down to me?"

"Mr. White's busy." I sip.

"Right. I get one new Cadillac a year. I thought I was worth more than that."

"I'm sure that Mr. White sees a lot of worth in you."

She sips from her drink and stares ahead, like she has forgotten I'm there. Then she starts talking without looking at me. "And I'm thinking maybe you are even a part of that gift." And then she looks at me as though she is disgusted. "Look what I traded my life for." She puts her drink down and reaches for a pack of cigarettes. She fumbles with it to get a cigarette out, and then she hands me a match and tells me, "Light my cigarette."

I do as I'm told and say, "Maybe, I ought to go."

Cheryl takes a puff and blows smoke ahead of her, and then she turns and blows smoke toward me. "Why do you think he's not here?"

"Who?"

"My husband, you dip shit," Cheryl says and stands up.

"I don't know."

With a cigarette in one hand and a drink spilling out of her other, she tells me. "Because it's boring as shit. So he's in San Antonio, in his apartment, playing like some cowboy come to town to buy most of it. And here I sit." She sucks on her cigarette. "Don't you wonder why he didn't give me my fan-fucking-tastic present? Why he isn't here, in person?"

"I'm young, Mam. I try not to think about those things."

"Well, it's not just what you're not thinking. It's that it's just so boring. He's got that bank. He's got his business interests. He's got Lord knows what else. And I got this."

"This don't look so bad," I say.

"I know. That's why I don't dare leave him. What else I got?" She looks at me like she's about to pounce on me, but I don't know if she'd pounce on me to tear off my clothes or beat the shit out of me. "Are you payment too? Is that what Sammy's thinking?"

Now I'm getting more than a little pissed. "I better be getting Mr. White's Cadillac."

"Sit down."

"I may be just a delivery boy, and I sure as hell am confused, but I can't help but thinking that me sitting down ain't going to do me or you no good."

She smiles. "You may regret not staying."

"I figure I'm going to have regrets no matter what I do now. So I'm just going to do what Mr. White told me to do."

She walks into the kitchen and comes with the straps of her purse slung over her forearm, she reaches into it and pulls out some keys. She flips them to me. "It's in the garage."

"Where's that?"

"Out the backdoor," and as I inch backward toward it, I try to memorize her standing there, puffing out smoke, swaying on her boot heels, sipping that drink, and looking like the very picture of my future regrets.

* * *

And so, just as I turn Mr. White's yellow Cadillac with the black vinyl top and the dark tinted windows out of the big gate and am kicking up dust because I got the heavy-foot, I see a pickup truck hauling ass behind me. I press the gas pedal harder, the truck closes in. As I'm looking in my rearview mirror, trying to see through the dust I'm kicking up, another pickup just suddenly appears in front of me. I see no roads, so the truck must have come cross country. I hit the horn. Then I hit the brakes to keep from running right up that pickup's ass. Then the other one pulls up right beside me. Dust is swirling all around us. I get out of the car, and yell, "Just what do you hillbillies, think you're doing?"

As the dust clears away, one man then another step out of the pickup trucks. The driver of the pickup now on the side of me has on a black suit, sunglasses, and slicked-back black hair. The other driver has on jeans, pointy-toed boots, a white shirt, and a straw cowboy hat. They look at me, then at each other, then in unison they duck into the cabs of their pickups. "Hey, who are you guys," I yell. One then the other comes out from the cabs of the pickups, and each one has a sawed-off shotgun. "You guys aren't cops are you?" I ask.

"Who are you?" the guy in the suit asks and points the sawed-off shot gun at me.

"*Quein es*?" the guy in the cowboy hat asks.

"I work for Mr. White."

"Where's he?" the black-suited man asks.

"At work. Where should he be?"

"You're a smart ass."

"Gringo child, why you have this car?" the man in the hat asks.

Then the sawed-off shot gun in the black-suited man's hands goes off, and I feel my shoulders jump up to me ears, and I jerk around to see a spray of holes ruining the yellow driver's door of Mr. White's Cadillac.

The man in the cowboy hat fires his and takes out the grillwork. They both pump their shotguns, shoot again, and the tires become shreds of rubber.

"What the hell do you two cretins think Mr. White is going to say?"

The man in the suit walks up to me, and I can see the beads of sweat on his forehead, and he puts his arm around my shoulder, and I can smell him growing a little rank in that black suit. "You tell 'Mr. White' what you seen. And you tell him it's a little greeting from Fred Carrasco. Mr. Carrasco don't talk shit and don't play games."

"How am I supposed to tell him when you just killed my ride?" And then I think that I may have just gotten myself killed.

With his arm around me, the black-suited man leads me to his pickup and opens the passenger side door. "Get in," he says.

"What's your name?" I ask.

"You don't need to know my name," he says. "Get in." And the other guy starts walking toward me. I can run. I can beg. I can try to fight two sawed-off shot guns. Instead, I get in.

The black-suited man comes around to the driver's seat and puts the sawed-off shot gun across the rifle rack. "Don't touch that," he says.

The first pickup pulls away, and we follow leisurely behind. "Mrs. White is sure going to be pissed."

"You seen her?" the man asks.

"Who? Was there a woman at the wreck?"

"Mrs. White, dip shit."

"Yeah. I brought her the new Cadillac Mr. White bought her and was bringing his back to him."

"I hear she's hot."

"She's all right."

"I mean, I hear she's so pissed off at him, she'll do anybody just to get back at him."

"I couldn't say."

"Could you guess?"

"I wouldn't want to."

"You got a mouth and an attitude." I waited for a bullet, but the man smiled. "You should be careful who you work for."

"So who do you work for?"

"You heard."

"Fred Carrasco is a gangster. What's he got to do with Mr. White?"

"You better shut up now."

"Well, what's your name?"

"You better shut up now." The man in the black suit turns to me and pulls down his sunglasses to stare at me over the tops of his glasses to be sure I got the point.

I shut up, for awhile. "So what if it wouldn't have been me?"

"Shut up."

"But, I mean, what if had been Mr. Sammy White in that car?"

"Shut the fuck up, you little shit ass." And I figure I had better shut up.

We drive to a gas station, and the man in the black suit nods to the attendant. He lowers his sunglasses, looks me up and down, and all but smiles. "You got a dime for a phone call?'

"You didn't rob me."

"You got balls, dip shit. Be careful you don't lose them," he says."

"Get out."

With my dime, I call the bank and get Hank Worley and the tone in his voice tells me I fucked up big time.

* * *

I sit on the coke machine—the long flat kind where you slide a soda water out of the rack—while I wait for somebody to pick me up. The attendant looks at me kind of strange. And I ask him how he knows the man in the black suit, but he says nothing. Then, after I eat a peppermint patty, peanuts, and some orange peanut butter crackers, Emmitt pulls up in his white Rambler.

"Oh Gregory," he says when I get in. "What have you done?"

"Nothing," I say.

"Well the, what has been done to you?"

I take my time telling Emmitt, and he shakes his head. And after I'm through with my story, I feel like I can't talk to Emmitt. So I just answer him "yes" and "no."

I had taken the bus that day, and so I ask Emmitt just to take me to the bus stop so I can catch it home. But he says he will get me home. When he pulls up in front of my house, he turns to me and says, "Gregory, be careful around Mr. White."

"Yes, sir?"

"Do you want me to explain anything to your parents?"

"No sir."

"Do you want to play tennis again?"

I feel myself smile. "Yes, sir," I say. Emmitt's old eyes look kind of watery to me, and he smiles, reaches across the seat, and pats my shoulder as I get out.

When I get out of the old Rambler, my father comes out of the house, looks at me, and says, "What you done?" And I turn from him to wave bye to Emmitt, who is waving rapidly to me from inside his Rambler.

* * *

I was lucky in that incident, but I proved to me and some others that I could hold my own. And people heard, and I got treated better. My mother and father talked to me more, asked me what I had decided to do with myself, asked if they could help me with whatever it was I had decided to do with myself. Mr. White didn't show up for several weeks. Some said he was hiding out, taking it on the lam. And of course, people knew who Fred Carrasco was. The tellers teased me, but they also sort of pampered me, gave me candy, bought me lunch from their homes. Hank Worley pumped me for as much information as he could get from me.

On the weekends, I played tennis with Emmitt, and I once even beat him a set. I saw our games as getting me in shape. So pretty soon it is August, and I know that I got to make some decisions. My future was running toward me. There was the draft, college, and my confusion. Emmitt voted for college and studying economics. He told me had friends at San Antonio College, said he would help me apply. He also told me that he hate to see me go to that nasty war. But then, Mr. White comes back to the bank and then to see me.

It is closing time for the bank, and since Emmitt starts to trust me more, I'm in the vault counting the money by myself. The bars and the timed door are open and in walks Mr. White. I turn and just see him, and my shoulders jump up to my ears. "Gregory," he says. "I owe you, and despite what some people say, I pay my debts."

"Mr White. I got your car blown up, so you really don't owe me nothing."

Mr. White shakes his head, then stares down at his shiny, ostrich skin boots. He takes his LBJ hat off with his right hand and puts it on top of the long row of steel drawers. He straightens out his tie, checks behind him, and keeps his left hand behind his back, like he's holding on to his ass. "Now, Gregory, a boy like you has a future with a fella like me. And I can watch out for your welfare."

"Yes sir. I like it just fine at the bank. I think I want to be a banker."

"I'm not talking about the bank," he says and checks around behind him again. He pulls his left hand from around his back. He's got this little travel case. He reaches in it and pulls out a Steves Bank money sack with what looks like a stack of bills inside. He puts it on the counter next to his hat. He reaches in again. He pulls out four sacks. "I know a lot of people. And from what I have heard about the way you operated around those tough vatos tried to intimidate me, well, I think you could make some money for me and yourself."

"How did you hear about what happened?"

"I know some birds. My wife also says good things." I stare at my toes. "Now these safes and such are filled with old money, right?"

"Schedule to be burned. That's what Emmitt tells me."

"Well then, what would be the harm of exchanging these bags of money for some of them that's in the safe?"

"Oh, I don't think so."

"You can count it. It's the same amount. No one's to know."

"Sir," I say and wish Emmitt is around.

"Like I say. You got a future, but it ain't here. You don't want to be a banker. Bankers hold other people's money."

"But you're a banker."

"I know people on the draft board, politicians, lawyers." He stares at me. I say nothing. "For my wife's sake, let's just exchange one sack for another." Looking at me, he grabs a fifteen-year-old sack of twenties. He puts his sack in its place, then reshuffles the sacks of money, and I let him. Then he stuffs another one of his sacks into the safe. After he is done, he comes to me and pats my shoulder. "You're a good man, Gregory."

"I ain't so good."

"Why don't you call the Feds tell them we got some money to burn. Tell them they should come by and pick it up."

"Emmitt usually makes that call."

"Why don't you do it?" And he stands there patting my shoulder, making me know I will do what he says, and I am mad at him and envious-like of him at the same time.

* * *

By the time that summer was over, I'd go right into Sammy's office. He'd close the door, and we'd discuss my future. He made calls and sent me out to interviews with friends of his. The guy he chose for me to work for was this redheaded, south side, "salesman." When Davy Wolf saw me and talked to me on my interview, he said, "Now with your looks and smooth talk, you can sell some Mexicans some refrigerators." So I did.

I sold refrigerators, cars, air conditioners, whatever Davy Wolf could find, to poor, scared illegals dodging immigration, ones just like Emilio and Tristina. Then Davy showed me the "horse" business. We'd go around to country horse auctions, buy the sick or old ones, and hire an acquaintance to truck them up to Canada where horse meat was legal. Short of it was, I became a salesman like Davy Wolf. Then I got drafted.

With my banking and sales experience, I became a paymaster at Da Nang. The biggest danger I had was from the black soldiers who wanted to beat the shit out of most white non-commissioned officers, especially paymasters. I talked my way to safety. And thinking like Sammy White and Davy Wolf, I found ways to pay myself a little extra.

When I got back, I resumed my career as a salesman and, with Sammy White's help, charged forward into my future or fate. I made more money than any banker, so I guess that I owed Sammy White, who eventually did some prison time. And I figure I never missed much by not going to college. And I guess I didn't miss much by not becoming a banker. But I figure I missed a lot by not keeping up my Saturday tennis games with ol' Emmitt.

First published in *descant* and winner of the 2012 Kay Cattarulla Short Story Award presented by the Texas Institute of Letters.

Lucas Jacobs

Hungarian Sonnet 1

You think that *paradicsom* is the fruit,
and fall in love again with naming. Here,
you cry, are people after my own heart,
who hang Eden and apple in one word, fat

on the tongue! But then you learn your "paradise"
is grown on a vine, and not on a branch—
a mere tomato, *száz forint* per bunch.
You comfort yourself: the early Rabbis

saw in Biblical fruit puns for desire
(citron) and destruction (carob); you note
what scholars now favor: pomegranate.
Gránátalma! It sounds to your ear

like a "soul stone." Ineffable, but hewn
down, somehow, still, and held tight in the hand.

First published in *Southwest Review*, volume 95, number 4, 2010

Tremor

When it started, she was still looking
for her face in the circle of water that
pooled every morning on the black granite
countertop. Somehow in the diurnal
ritual of coffee and toast she created
always this small puddle that stilled into
the only mirror she trusted to start her
days. It always needed a moment for her

features to pull into focus; she'd mistake
the reflection of a track light for a glint
in her eye, or find a new beauty mark
in a crumb on the skim of the water. This

35

time, before her eyes could find her eyes
the floor pulled loose and set the puddle
running like a river to a waterfall at the edge
of the granite. She was just able, for one

second, to see what she had found of her
flesh elongate, stretched from chin to
sandy hair into little more than a thread,
and vanish at the end of the counter. She
gasped, and threw both hands forward to
grasp the granite—not to keep from falling,
not in mind of the earthquake's power to
cast her like a doll onto the floor, or

to call down a hail of plaster and pans and
fixtures freed from the ceiling into gravity,
not in the need to get to the door, not even
aware of the temblor at all, not yet: she held
herself up, shut her eyes, and opened them so
that there would be before her simply a trickle
of water, not a quicksilver looking-glass
carrying her right off the edge of the world.

First published in *The Evansville Review*, Volume XXIII, 2013

Matthew Pitt

Lousy with Light

I've reached that moment of moving day when I bestow any item that failed to earn its way into the U-Haul—we're talking pizza pans, oscillating fans, even occasional floor lamps—to my neighbors. I've donated such departing gifts my entire urban life; six-and-a-half moves, all told (partially counting eight stopgap weeks spent crammed in a broom closet).

This time around, though? Not a soul lives beneath me. And as for my upstairs neighbor?

Simon has already taken quite enough.

If I said the name Simon Rowe beside you, would it set off dread bells? Simon is a famous children's singer. Famous with audiences, in other words, who drown in shrieks of laughter upon witnessing bodily functions, and whose tastes rise and set around the virtues of sugar cereals. You may have had the misfortune of hearing Simon on TV, or piped into mall and roller-skating rink speaker systems. But unless you've lived *with* his nasal voice above you, his songs worming through air vents or the gap in your ceiling, you don't fully get it.

Boy, did I get it. I've heard Simon's entire insipid repertoire, from "Three-Second Rule" and "What's a Why?" to "Big Rude Bagel" ("*So big for little hands to follow, so chewy for small mouths to swallow*"). Heard him on guitar, harmonica and hurdy-gurdy, kettledrum and piccolo. His apartment doubles as a kindermusik studio: He works with parents who home-school. They release their broods to his care two hours at a time. All so Simon can chirp relentless rounds and practice new material in their presence, then teach the kids to butcher harmonies all their own. On every school day, from morning until afternoon, the building gasps and quakes with shrieks, scuffling feet, soggy noses, ragged chords, and thumping so insidious, I now consider the average jackhammer jockey, carving pavement, to possess a percussive touch worthy of Puente.

Initially I took solace (fine: *schadenfreude*) in the modest dimensions of Simon's apartment—about 50 square feet less than mine. But then I started noticing full-color posters plastered on city buses, bearing Simon's wild-eyed grin; giant billboards in the theatre district;

morning-show appearances. Turns out he commutes from a palatial suburban estate; this is only his "education annex."

I work at home too—a freelance editor. But with Simon's kiddy cavalcade, I couldn't focus on projects. Yes, I put on headphones, but only heavy metal could mute the rainmaking upstairs: it's one thing to pump iron to Iron Maiden, quite another to restructure tech-heavy text to it. My gig pool evaporated. Then the economy followed suit. Simon's songs grew more painfully bright, as my cash flow dimmed. Before I knew it, I couldn't afford to break my lease.

That's not the worst of what Simon inflicted.

Last month, I prepared an elaborate first anniversary dinner for my sweetheart. To procure the proper ingredients, I hit scads of grocery stores and specialty markets. By the time I reached the boutique candle shop, I had to remind myself she deserved this show of devotion, fully and without grumble. That eating in was my idea, and my attempt at being frugal.

But with each long register line, stalled train, and swipe of my card's magnetic strip, panic pinched my ribs: here I was casting off cash in spurts I couldn't spare, and forsaking moments of apartment silence I should have hoarded, to scrape together a living. At my desk was an article for a second-tier outdoors glossy, about differences between thorns, spines, and prickles in plants. Turn it around quick, and I could be sure and cover rent. Fail to follow through...

It didn't matter. Sweetheart's presence was worth any amount of scurrying and Visa debt. Her arrival, her hopeful smile as she praised the table settings and hovering scents, confirmed my choice. I wrung tension from my hands; told my headache to beat it. This night needed to not be held hostage by anxiety, or glimpses of dread. It was for celebrating a year together, and hinting with hope at our years ahead.

But while savoring course two, with duck confit still to come, bursts of whistling like portents sounded above us.

"Hey, is that your neighbor playing? That sweet kids' singer?"

It was: he'd lingered later than normal.

"He won *five* children's Grammies the other night," my girl reported, beaming. "You know what they call children's Grammies? The Jammies."

A forkful of corn mache hovered near my dear's lip. I suddenly wanted to snatch it, suddenly thought she wasn't worthy of the effort put into it.

"I visited his place once," I said instead, scuffling away. "To borrow a flashlight during an outage. There wasn't one CD in his entire apartment. No wonder he cranks out rapid vapid verses—he's insulated from any accomplished music that might shame him into stopping."

"Ffft. He probably just went digital."

I opened the oven, fetching the fowl. "Oh, you're defending him?"

On some level, I knew she wasn't. But by then, even neutral remarks about Simon stabbed at me. By then, after all, I'd bludgeoned him with a vast assortment of heavy wishes: that the city's D.A. would divulge some dark secret about the guy; that his commuter line would derail; a shorting amp, electrocute him. I'd thought myself into a box of disgust, one the girl I loved was now sealing me inside.

"I know this song, the one he's whistling now," she cried. *"Hair can't brush itself, you know. Legs can't scrub their knees. Teeth can't floss themselves, you know, so it's up to you and me."*

"Stop."

"We've got to have Simon sign a CD for us."

"I said stop."

"Too soon, you think? Maybe you're right." If we wait and have him sign it once we start a family...give it to our kids when they..."

Then it came: a discharged thunderclap I couldn't avert or contain. "Kids? If Simon sings the kind of saccharine shit you want them listening to, there won't *be* kids in our goddamn future!"

Down went the baking dish. Down went that beautifully cooked bird.

The rest of what I ate that night, and have eaten since, I've eaten alone.

When I first found this apartment listing—placed by the prior tenant—it claimed the space was "lousy with light." I saw that description and got excited: few first-floor apartments lay claim to much sunlight. I read those words with naïveté. Not as an editor, who should be attuned to trick phrasings, double meanings.

The lousy light was none other than my neighbor above.

Who, the next day, jiggered out a tune with his kinder-troupe, one impossible for me to shrug off: *Well there might be a wall between us, doesn't mean we can't be buddies. No need to act nasty, neighbor, no need to growl all crazy-nutty.* See? Simon *did* take something from me. And no way he's thanking me in his eventual Jammie acceptance speech.

Anyway, my lease ceases at midnight. I turned in my keys. Thanks for listening. Say there, any interest in taking a breadmaker off my hands? Won't have room for it where I'm headed next, but I promise, it heats beautifully...

Nat O'Reilly

Unheard

Immigrants suffocating
in an abandoned
Hanjin shipping container
baking in the midday sun
at a remote rest area
beside a first-world highway
beat on the steel walls
and shout desperately
in their native tongue
but they are too far away
from the restrooms
and vending machines

Houston

I took an eight-hour-round-trip drive
to spend six hours drinking in Houston
with expat mates. We stuffed ourselves
with corn chips and *enchiladas verdes*
and sipped on big-ass margaritas
while knocking back Texas-sized
shots of tequila provided gratis
by waitresses with enhancements.

At the faux British pub near the university,
we drank Bass and Guinness served
by college girls wearing short shorts
and Ugg boots while discussing
the distance the iconic Ugg has travelled
from the western suburbs of Sydney
and the back seats of Toranas and Falcons
to the pages of *Vogue*, the display windows
of up-market department stores
and the carefully-maintained feet
of affluent American daughters

shuffling across the campuses
of expensive private universities.

At *The Big Easy Social and Pleasure Club*
geriatric cowboys mixed with homeboys
and posturing hombres from the barrio
as cowgirls and divas two-stepped
and swung to the funk laid down
by the five-piece-band fronted
by a sister who shook her money-maker
like she'd been shakin it all her life.
We leant on the bar drinking Fosters
from oil cans "brewed" in Fort Worth,
laughing quietly at ourselves.

Moumin Quazi

Stuck in the Mud

The rain's early sprinkle had already created a post-dusty film on Clint Clay's old pickup truck's broad windshield. The mottled dust merely spread across the glass as the wipers slowly slid up and over and back down in an almost annoying repetition. Clint thought, Damn, I wish had refilled that wiper fluid. In the meantime, he simply had to wait for the sprinkle to work itself up into a harder rain, so that the window would finally clean itself as he made his way along the dirt road that minutes ago had been hard and dry. Now, it was beginning to soften up. At first Clint welcomed the way the sprinkle held the dust down on the road; but, now as the remaining light of day retreated westward, it was hurried along by a deep purplish bank of storm clouds, prematurely darkening the sky and the view ahead. An occasional stab of lightning followed by an ever closer rumble signaled to Clint that his life was about to get messy, and quickly. He still had another sixty-nine or so miles to go before he arrived at the large tin-roofed shed that served as a shelter and depot where he housed emergency stores and feed for his livestock, a few dozen head of Brangus cattle.

It had been a temperate fall this year, but that didn't lessen his gratitude for the rain, the further relief from a previously record-breaking drought and a further buffer from the devastating wildfires that had ravaged thousands of square miles of ranchland across the State. In those fires, Clint had lost 30 head, and he was forced to sell off an additional hundred head back East at a regrettable loss. Tonight, he was making sure the store of hay and feed he had amassed for the upcoming winter was protected. But now, for the last twenty-or-so miles, the rain had evolved into an insistent downpour, forcing Clint to slow down and pick his way through the ever-increasing slog. The bed of his pickup was heavy with supplies and a few covered bales of hay. The tarpaulin that he had tied down still held firm, he saw, and that relieved him.

It was while he was looking at his rear-view mirror to check on the tarp that his truck slid off the road, jerking his steering wheel out of his hands for a second. He hit the brakes and came to a stop just off the shoulder and into a slight dip. It wasn't a ditch, and he checked to make sure he hadn't hit a railing or tree or fence-post. "Goddammit!" Clint said, hitting the steering wheel with both hands as if he was shoving away a bully at the bar. He righted the wheel as he pressed the accelerator pedal, but the truck only wiggled frustratingly and jarringly from side to side, barely inching forward in the rut he found himself in. "Shee-it," he whispered. "Sheeit, sheeit, shit."

He reached under the passenger seat and grabbed a heavy duty flashlight. He then fished a folded-up rain poncho from his extended cab behind the seat. Muttering under his breath, he pulled the plastic over his denim jacket, put his cowboy hat back on and got out of the warmth and dryness of his truck. His boot sunk into the now water-filled crap-track his truck had just sloppily carved into the shoulder of the road.

He went 'round the back and saw what he had suspected: his right back tire was indeed stuck in the mud. And the rain continued to fall on him and on through the halogen beam of his Maglite. "It's gonna be a long night," he said, "because sooner or later some fool is gonna write a story about this inconsequential incident, and readers will wonder, "What the hell was the point of THAT?"

Sidney Thompson

The Liars Notebook

"Buyers are liars." That was the main thing New Cars Sales Manager Jimmy Bertella told Cooper to remember, so that was the first thing Cooper wrote in his pocket-size spiral notebook. Then Cooper jotted, "Never say, 'Can I help you?'" Jimmy said the cocksuckers will refuse the help they need and lie every time, telling you, "I'm not buying today. I'm just looking." Instead, Jimmy instructed him to say, "Are you looking for something like the car you drove up in or something different this time?" And if the cocksucker was to say it again, "I'm just looking," like Cooper didn't hear him the first time, then Cooper was to have the balls to stand up to the motherfucker and say, "Are you looking for a car, truck, van, or SUV? And would that be new or pre-owned? It's a big lot here at Hank Hood Automall, so let me point the way."

Other miscellanies:

Say "pre-owned," not "used"

"Special program," not "lease"

When out of ideas, say, "I've got a great idea, follow me," and get a T.O.

T.O. = turn over an up to any manager or senior salesman

Up = customer

Time is death to a deal.

Never answer a question without redirecting with a question.

Always remove sunglasses before greeting customers.

Free lunch on Saturdays

Cooper also watched videos on the eight steps to a sale. On his third day of training, during lunch, he test drove a 5-speed Pontiac Solstice, Mysterious Black, with the top down. He called in advance, and his wife waved from their balcony.

"How's it ride?" She tossed him the sandwich he'd made but forgotten, wrapped in foil.

Cooper smiled into the sun. "Like the Bat Mobile!" But it rode rough, as if on wagon wheels. "What do you think?"

She grinned as though she understood this car right here right now was his promise he'd make real money soon. That unemployment was a mere holiday of the past. That they were on their way to being approved for the very thing she'd come to believe most important: a house, a sanctuary, a hiding place with their name on it.

They rarely had sex anymore that wasn't Ambien-induced, and she always wore leotards and dance dresses around the apartment before and after work at the Fairhope Dance Studio across the alley. So limber. Fourteen percent body fat.

Since selling her apartment in New York two years ago to move to Alabama and get married, she'd grown quieter in stages. Then, last year, her panic attack, disguised as a heart attack—the palpitations, the faintness, the pulsing numb and pain in her left arm. Only moments, on the highway, after spending Thanksgiving weekend with Cooper's parents. Three whole days with Henry and Jewel.

Cooper pushed his sunglasses back up his sweating nose, then honked and, so cutely, newly, she honked, deep from within her throat. Her clothes like a foiling skin. Then he took the shifts to the spine back to work.

First published in *Connu*, Fall 2013

Chemical

This was the type of deal Finance Manager Kim Mickel was still in the business for. He scanned over the old lady's bureaus from Transunion and Equifax to gather a sense of her. Although on scores alone Elnetta Johnson was an eye-popping bullet in anybody's book, she'd be an automatic decline if he shot her to any bank as she truthfully was, with no valid driver's license and making only $613 a month from Social Security. And not any bank would buy a loan with a ghost cosigner, but since her grandson had a license, he was instrumental.

Getting proof of income waived was the easy part. With her scores, no bank would question the $4,178 monthly retirement that Kim added to her application. To explain the pesky deficiencies, though, he had to come up with a story, the best possible story. It was his storytelling ability that got most of his deals funded. It's what paid his bills. It's what exhilarated his feeble heart. Why people ever began calling him "Chemical" in the first place so many years ago.

Oh, yeah, thought Kim, considering Marquis's age. That was the key. That was it. That was it!

Kim made edits to the Credit App. Marquis Gray wasn't a welder. He struck through that. No, Mr. Gray was a student who still lived with his grandmother. She was putting him through college, but because of

46

her age, her poor eye sight, she couldn't drive, so she had no use for a license. But she had use for a car, of course, and Marquis was her driver. The car was for her, to replace the one that had just recently quit on her. He was simply going to drive it for her, drive her to church, drive her to the grocery store, and drive her to the doctor. You know, the usual. No, there was no straw purchase here. Nothing unethical. The car was purely for Ms. Elnetta Johnson. That's right. For Elnetta Johnson.

But after taking a look at the incentives on Yukons, he revised his story. It wasn't a car she needed. She needed an SUV, something with enough space for her wheel chair and for her plants. She was always asking her grandson to run her to the nursery and buy flowers and plants. She was a retired botanist, you know. And botany just so happened to be Mr. Gray's major.

So that's how he structured the deal. Ms. Elnetta Johnson and Mr. Marquis Gray on a 2013 Yukon SLT, because Ms., no, *Dr., yes, Dr.* Johnson expected and deserved the finest.

First published in *Beetroot*, Fall 2013

Sybil Pittman Estess

Squirrel

1

I always hated when Daddy had been
doing that. They were too fat, and
he cooked them with white rice.
But we did not question what father
said or served. He liked to cook.
There were no vegetables with "the mess."
And birds had little pocks where shot.
Broken blood vessels, meat bloody.
We would chew and swallow, silent.
(The bullets had all been picked out.)

2

My son said he killed many with
his BB and then air guns. All just
here and there around our Houston
house. We never saw them. Once,
he said he hit a bird—and he wrote
a poem about that death in high school.
He cried. Now he is doing the 12 Steps.
Number 4 in a moral inventory of his
thirty-three years. In writing. It's long.

Parting

In their small Mississippi hometown, my husband hugs his brother.
Pats his face in the casket. "Don't leave me now. Please don't!" he weeps.
Bees killed Roy. He was mowing on a tractor. He died in ten minutes.
Before the funeral, three days later, we went to see his body. No wake,
no family gathers in one of the several private, formal, available funeral
home rooms. Roy's body is stored in an office, "to keep it cooler." One
woman clerk keeps coming in, pulling out drawers, banging and
fumbling to get paperclips or staples. I am irate. The man running the

place, Jimmy Boyd, in his drawl says, "It's time t'git on go. We gotta load him up fer the church. Once there, hundreds wait to see. No chance for only two brothers to be alone, only offspring. It is nearly a state funeral in a country town. Seven eulogies. First my husband's, then the Director of NASA's, the astronauts' and on and on. One had been on Apollo 13. It all lasts three hours. After the procession to the burial, there's fried chicken, ham, peas, cornbread, homemade cakes at the church hall. All I could think about was that before, back at the house, I had asked my spouse if he wanted to go to Roy alone, if he wanted to be alone at all with the man he called "Bro." No Then, once there, what I saw when we got to the cold office that held the body in a box was bloodless, pale, stopped cold. Roy was always on the move. His blood ran hot. And his hair was not parted correctly, the way he really wore it. But straight back, combed by his son. Roy always part it on the right side.

On Leaving the Lake: 9,000 feet

We came in summer heat, through
drought and no campfires allowed.

We stayed through two weeks of Indian
fall with Aspen so gold and red they

could have been butter and fire. No rain,
so leaves lingered. My two bought trees

have not turned. I watered them daily.
Hummingbirds migrated to Mexico.

Yesterday, first snow on Rocky peaks.
Geese are paused on the lake. Crows

caw for the start of cold. Moose are now
sleuthing and elk are mostly across roads

in the National Park, hiding from hunters.
My red geraniums still bloom, the purple

petunias we have to leave. No freezes
have come, although three fall frosts.

Fields are brown, ground cover is red.
Cafes and shops in town lock their doors.

Stores are beginning to sport skis, snow-
mobiles. Although I am still swimming daily

in the main lodge's heated pool, it closes
next week. Time to leave? Who can board

up this gorgeous plenty? We will drive south
now, to family, friends—what we call home.

Terri Tucker

Preacher Man

Everyone has a first crush or a first love. Mine was Big George's second son, Mike. His sandy brown hair and intense blue eyes attracted me, but the fact that I was ten, and that our fathers were co-workers, co-drinkers and our mothers were co-enablers directed our destiny.

We led parallel lives: each family had six kids, our grandparents had local land holdings, our parents had survived the Great Depression and had suffered the aftermath. Nevertheless, our fathers had strong work ethics, and alcoholism was the glue that held or dissolved our family dynamics. Our paths crossed often during a two year period.

Despite these, our families didn't share religions. My parents split their religious affiliations between my father's Catholic legacy, shrouded in a rosary, and my mother's Baptist congregation member-ship, swaddled in her Cradle Roll enrollment. Her mother, Grandma, intervened, either to be nosy or to encourage our church attendance. So we bounced from a small west-side missionary church with its musty basement to Grandma's grand east-side red brick Baptist Church with its stained-glass windows.

On the other hand, Mike's parents had no regular religious influence, except the legacy from his maternal grandparents who were Methodists and his paternal side's sporadic affiliation with nondenominational churches.

Nevertheless, our connection paled when his father was called to preach. Yes, Big George was a charismatic preacher, of the nondenominational variety. My father may have served as an altar boy at the Catholic Church in Spofford, but he had no desire for formal preaching. After parochial school took its toll on him, he was religioned "out." Except for religious music; he encouraged us to play "The Old Rugged Cross" and "Softly and Tenderly" on the keyboard along with Marty Robbins' "Street of El Paso."

Looking at Big George's hulking body, you couldn't see his religion. But he had religion. If his hands moved, he spread the Word through his motions and embraces. If his mouth moved, he spoke the Holy words, the Holy message. On the right day, of course.

His tall frame overshadowed everyone and his loud sober voice, when he was sober, called you close as he embraced you, or sent you to flee if it was tainted with drink of the devil. Usually dressed in bib overalls with one strap hanging down and dangling on one side, he looked more like a small-time dirt farmer in this dusty south Texas community.

Slicked back, his once velvet black hair was now sprigged with long strands of gray, damp with hair cream while his large jowls and cheeks reeked of Aqua Velva shaving lotion. Big George defined the televangelist look long before the contemporary television market did. In fact, he could have served as the model for a televangelist poster.

But when he spoke you knew: he was a preacher. A home-grown, self-professed-gospel preacher. What he lacked in a seminary education, he oozed in enthusiasm of a newly converted sinner who was driven to share the good news. It had saved him from sundry sins. Anew with holiness, in addition to his burning compassion for all people, he needed to spread the word. Spread the gospel.

He spent long hours sharing the message. Early to rise, he prepared, prayed, pondered, before he perused the neighborhood. If he could get redemption and salvation, and it was free, he could, by golly, spread it around and share it with all the other poor folks.

Big George was brassy, commanding, and his message the same: fire and brimstone, hell and damnation. And more hell than the others.

Within earshot of Big George, you could follow a trail of "I love you Jesus. Oh Lord, give me words. Save me. Forgive me." At times, he choked on his own tears. Recovering his breath after his big hand fondled a crumpled handkerchief across his face, he continued, "Help me serve you. Sinners, repent today. Be forgiven—God loves you. Devil, get thee behind me. Oh, we are Sinners. Lord, we are Sinners. Turn your back on Satan. Follow Jesus."

These mantras plus a combination of stand-by Bible verses followed him, as his slow gait and his big bellowing sermonettes attracted followers. We didn't have to wait for a traveling preacher or tent revival to come to the town: we had Big George.

Able to captivate an audience or at least keep local gawkers awake, Big George could preach on the street, in a makeshift tent, in the Westside missionary church, or in front of his Dairy King eatery. With its tattered cover, his Bible looked comfortable, swaddled like an infant by his large hands. With an unusual deftness his oil stained fingers readily turned to the gospel, and located apt verses about sinning, forgiveness, and being born again. His quick access to scriptures was impressive; one of his favorites was from the book of Acts, chapter two, verse thirty-eight: "Repent and be baptized, every one of you, in the name of Jesus Christ for the forgiveness of your sins. And you will receive the gift of the Holy Spirit."

To better serve the public he extended worship services right on the spot: his local hamburger joint conveniently served as an open air church. Big George would easily slip away from the grill and preach to local diners seated on the benches of the picnic tables. He shook many hands, hugged many women, pinched many babies' cheeks, and invited all to return for another sermon.

Whether they were willing to listen or not, they wouldn't dare leave their burger and fries meal until he finished his sermon. The overflow galley of prospective followers sat on the thin folding chairs, or sat on the ground under the oak trees.

At the height of his preacher career, Big George, by invitation, would fill in for preachers at the nondenominational church. There his followers and local church goers would benefit from padded pews and heating and cooling. His ability to draw a crowd enticed local religious leaders to embrace him, temporarily. His charisma could boost their straggly attendance on any given Sunday.

In addition to his calling to preach, to save fellow heathens and to spread the word of Jesus, Big George had one natural calling: to cook. His hamburger, fries, beans, and barbeque could melt anyone's resistance to his overbearing message. His cooking was saturated in memorable flavor and grease and blessed by prayer. The burger's paper sleeve had a tell-tale stain of oil, and the large, toasted hamburger buns were crisp on the edges and their tops glistened with a smear of grease. Mayo or mustard just added a color tint to the sheen.

Big George's Dairy King was nestled under oak trees and close to a historic school yard on the west side of town. His family owned property west of the city limits, on a rocky jut of a hill above the old cemetery. He circled back and forth from the family homestead to the hamburger joint. He opened up most days, but just as patrons settled into a lunch routine of burgers, fries and soda, and just as his clientele grew into the huge crowds before a local Friday night football game, he'd disappear.

At times, his wife would cover and his two older sons kept the window open and the grill smoking. Betty had stayed by his side despite the lean years, the frequent unemployment and the half dozen children to feed. From a prominent family, her father had been a local doctor who had died decades earlier during the nefarious flu epidemic of 1918.

Their oldest daughter, who was my best friend during elementary school, was crippled from a childhood bout with polio. According to the locals, Big George had delayed or denied her medical care for years but later allowed her to be treated at one of the Shriner's Children's Hospital. During those years, Big George, defied most medical maladies and denied treatment. Instead, he treated ailments with home remedies or prayer. It didn't seem to matter whether he was practicing religion or heathenism at the time.

Being good friends with Vicky was my connection to the family, to their dysfunction, plus it sustained my crush on Mike. Being the second son, he was more sympathetic and helpful to his sister and eager to help her when her wheelchair stuck in loose gravel or wouldn't roll through grassy paths under the huge oak trees around the Dairy King.

Mike was friendly, sweet, and knew his charm and looks would be his ticket out of Big George's grip. But for the meantime, he played his part and worked hard and obeyed the family patriarch. Whether it was up on the hill at his grandmother's Lanny's or at the burger joint, all three boys worked from an early age.

Their family was as much a migrant family as the field workers' families in South Texas. They may not leave town for long but their business could be thriving one day and then no one knew where they were the next. Often, the townspeople drove up to place their order only to find the joint closed and sliding window locked. Despite the fact that Big George built up preacher reputation as well as his business at the burger joint, didn't mean he was loyal to either. If he landed a job as a rough neck or a driller, his unpredictable actions and quick itch to leave town won out.

If the Dairy King was closed for long, it meant Big George had fallen off the wagon and found Lone Star and oil rigs with bigger paychecks, which were more rewarding than preaching the Word, baptizing dirty sinners, and flipping greasy burgers.

For many years, my dad and uncles, along with Big George, worked in the Texas oil fields. We were all nomadic, moving after one night's shift notice because either the rig was shutting down for a couple of weeks, or other oil companies were drilling new wells and needed crews. In the 50s and early 60s, it was about length of jobs, the next job not about benefits. Heeding the call from a new driller and moving several hundred miles west to Sonora, Odessa or Midland area was the norm.

Our family traveled the same path; we too, left our hometown for a few years before returning for my sophomore year of high school. Again,

I was able to rekindle my dear friendship with Vicky and reconnect with Big George's family. The oldest son, George Jr. had graduated, and Mike was a senior in high school. Even though we were old acquaintances, Mike had become somebody in high school and was dating a popular girl, a twirler, whose father was a well-to-do realtor.

I knew I didn't have a chance with him. But when we were away from school, at the makeshift churches or the burger place, he would be attentive. Climbing the social ladder, Mike was struggling to free himself from the booming preacher of a father and find his own path.

Based on our families' legacy, we knew what we had to do: work. Work and more work. That was our fate. After high school graduation we could leave home to work or to leave home to marry.

As the youngest sophomore in my class, only fourteen, I never went out with Mike. He never asked me for a real date. But we rode home together, ran errands for our families, and picked up his sister at school or at her grandmother's. We were thrown together by fate, by negligence, by alcohol. Isn't it funny that alcoholism wasn't mentioned during that time, and the label dysfunctional families must have been hidden between the pages of a psychology text book.

One evening he managed a quick kiss before I went inside, and I at that moment I daydreamed that he would dump the popular girl for me. But, his teasing about us getting married some day may have been the turning point. By then Daddy and Mama knew about my infatuation; however, it took me awhile to realize what must have happened: Daddy talked to Big George and warned him. After that Mike never looked at me. So much for first crushes. (But he didn't marry the twirler, either.)

By then Big George was back at the Dairy King but wasn't preaching. He still drew big crowds at lunch, but the bigger his success the quicker he backpedaled to the oil field or moved Betty around the country to one small South Texas town after another. They bounced from Pearsall to Encinal and to Sandia, living most of this time in a truck with a camper shell. Other times, they simply disappeared, the two of them, and left the younger kids.

They'd leave them with Big George's mother, Lanny, on the hill at the edge of town. They were always fed and sent to school but I doubt if they ever felt connected to their parents. They were absent in so many ways.

We went different directions. Mike's sisters finished their college education after some time, and George Jr. and Mike landed steady jobs with the state highway department. I was proud when they retired after working their way up with the state.

They didn't inherit Big George's itch to wander or preach. Instead of alcohol and other vices, they focused on family. Big George and Betty faded deeper into the anonymity of South Texas. No one heard much from them during their last years. Not even their children.

Now three of the six siblings are deceased. George Jr. and a younger brother Ronnie died within a short span of each other; my dear friend Vicky died this past spring.

At George Jr's funeral, I looked across the aisle at the remaining family members. Awash with the past, I remembered the strength we children found in each other. We needed each other during those unstable times, we bonded in friendship, and we managed to weather the storms. Despite the anguish of growing up, the trials of dysfunctional families, the negative community judgment, we all worked through those years. At times, we made it on a wing and a prayer. Maybe the Preacher Man's prayers were answered.

As far as first crushes, they are like childhood—important—yet fleeting. Later in high school, I walked into a locally owned burger joint on the north side of town, and with Roy Orbison belting out "Pretty Woman" on the juke box, I met my real love.

Terry Dalrymple

Not Meanin' to Shoot Myself

Third time's the charm, that's how the saying goes, Jason thought as the girl slid into his passenger seat. A charmer himself, he hadn't much considered the saying before because he'd never needed a third time—or even a second. The first time had always been his charm. But he considered it now and desperately hoped that it was true.

A natural-born flirt since grade school, he had always been attractive to women of all ages. Now forty-seven, he had lately—only lately—had two swings and two misses due to no fault of his own that he could conceive (though his aversion to contemporary pop music might have contributed to the first of the two). But now, here was this girl, Mandy—no, Mindi, he reminded himself, with two i's (over which she no doubt drew little hearts instead of dots)—sliding into the passenger seat of his Audi A6—jet black, with four doors because he sometimes chauffeured his clients—her short black skirt scrunching farther up her thighs, dangerously close to revealing whatever she wore—or didn't wear—underneath. She flashed him a white-toothed smile and blushed when he complimented her legs.

"Beautiful," he said. "Perfect. Like a model's."

Still blushing, she looked down at her legs, then back at him. "Actually," she said, "I'm going to be an anchor woman."

Doubtful, he thought, but he smiled back at her. "You'll make a beautiful one." I'll watch you every night."

She giggled and patted his shoulder. "You're so sweet."

She'd said that when he offered her a ride, too. "You're so sweet"—a sure sign that the third time would, indeed, be the charm.

He had met her at Vinny's Vino Bar. Vinny, whose real name was Wacy Ballinger and who haled from an east Texas farming family, had bought both the bar and his home through Jason when he moved to McKinney. He had planned to name the establishment Wacy's Watering Hole, but Jason had convinced him that a trendier name would attract both a larger and a better class of clientele. Vinny did, in fact, happen to stock a few fine wines, but otherwise there was nothing particularly *vino* about the bar. Vinny sold more beer and mixed drinks than wine, and the trendy frozen sweet drinks he concocted sold especially well to his young female client base. That's what Mandy—no, Mindi, damn it, Mindi, Mindi, Mindi!—had been drinking when Jason first spotted her.

That Friday after work—his charm had led him naturally into selling high-end real estate, both residential and commercial—he stopped in for a comfort drink after losing, for the first time in his career, an especially lucrative sale.

Vinny delivered his drink. "Feelin' alright?"

Jason shook his head. "Not feelin' too good myself."

Vinny chuckled." "It's a song, right?"

"Right. But unfortunately, it's also the truth."

"Maybe this'll help. He set the Crown and Coke on a cardboard coaster. "And there's more where that came from."

From his corner table, Jason scanned the room but spotted no familiar faces. Then he scanned the bar, and there sat the girl, an empty bar stool on either side of her. She pursed her full lips and sucked a straw full of colorful frozen dink into her mouth. She swallowed, then checked her phone. She turned to check the entrance. Obviously frustrated, she checked the phone again, then pursed her lips for another suck at the straw. Jason rose and walked casually to the bar stool on her left. When he set his drink on the bar, the girl glanced over at him.

"I'm sorry," he said. "Is this spot taken?"

She shook her head. "Apparently not."

He sat. "Damn," he said, "as pretty as you are you surely didn't get stood up."

She shrugged, finished a sip through the straw. "Sort of. I mean, not exactly. Just some girl friends." She returned her attention to the straw and sucked up the remains of her drink, the straw gurgling as the glass ran dry.

"Can I buy you another?" Jason asked.

She shrugged again. "Why not? Doesn't look like I'm going anywhere."

"What are you drinking?"

"Mango-Watermelon Daiquiri."

"Of course." Jason repressed a shudder. "Those are good, aren't they?"

"Really good," she said. "Especially because you can't taste the alcohol."

"Right. That's what you want in a good drink for sure." He motioned to Vinny, who, seeing that Jason had moved to the bar, smiled slyly and walked their way. "Another Mango-Watermelon Daiquiri for the lovely lady." Here he paused. "I'm sorry." He lay his right palm very gently against the middle of her back. "I don't know your name." I'm Jason.

"Mindi," she said, "with two *i*'s, no *y*."

"I love that name. It's as beautiful as you are."

She giggled and grinned, showing a mouthful of very white teeth. "Thanks."

He patted her lightly, then removed his hand from her back and turned back to Vinny. "Another Mango-Watermelon Daiquiri for Mindi and another Crown and Coke for me."

Mindi scrunched up her face. "Eew."

"I know," Jason said. "You can taste the alcohol. But it's been a rough day. I need something strong."

She shrugged. "Whatev'. Sorry about your day."

"Sounds like you're having a rough one, too."

She sucked on her straw, then said, "Sort of. I mean, the day was okay, but tonight's not looking so good." She checked her phone, looked toward the door. "I mean, they were supposed to meet me here, my friends. We graduated from college together two years ago. But we stay in touch, you know, and we were supposed to meet here for a drink before grabbing some dinner and then going to the Atomic. Do you know that club? It's great. This band, The Crabmasters, they're playing there tonight. I swear, they sound just like Coldplay, probably even better. They're great." Finally she stopped and looked at Jason. "I'm sorry. Sometimes I talk too much."

He smiled reassuringly. "Not at all. You have a lovely voice. I like listening to you."

"Thanks." She flashed him another white smile. "You're nice. You remind me of my grandpa."

In mid-sip of his Crown and Coke, he struggled not to choke. He managed to swallow without incident. "Your grandpa, huh?"

"Yeah. He likes to listen to me, too. And he's really nice, like you."

He switched the subject back to her evening plans. Her car was in the shop, so her mother had dropped her at Vinny's on her way to yoga class, and Mindi was to ride with her friends from there. She lived with her mother while she—Mindi—looked for a job, which, besides working at a donut shop near her mother's apartment part-time, she hadn't yet found. Her mother lived in an apartment because her—Mindi's—father had left when she—Mindi—was seven and she—Mindi's mother—

couldn't afford to keep the house. But she—Mindi's mother—was doing quite well these days and had begun thinking about buying a house, which Mindi hoped she'd do because she—Mindi— wanted a dog—a teacup poodle—but the apartment didn't allow it.

"Don't you just love them?" she said. "Tea cup poodles. OMG, they're so freaking cute. I could eat them up."

He said he did. He said they were his favorites. "My ex and I," he said, "we had one. But she—my ex, I mean—left me for a guitar player—I don't remember the name of his band—and she took Fifi with her. I don't miss my ex so much anymore, but, God, I miss that little dog."

"Aww," Mindi said and slid off her bar stool. She wrapped her arms around his neck and squeezed. She kissed his cheek. "I'm so sorry. That's so sad."

"Thanks," he said. "That felt good." And he realized that he meant it. The hug had felt spontaneous, it had felt sincere, it had felt sympathetic. He actually did have an ex, and they actually had owned a dog, a chocolate lab named Rex, and she actually had taken the dog when she left him—not for a guitar player but for a computer geek on his way to New York for a six-figure position in an up-and-coming communications operation. His ex had been ten years his junior, and despite his frequent philandering—he just couldn't help himself—he did, honestly, adore her, and he did love that chocolate lab. It had all come back as he invented the Fifi story, and Mindi's sympathetic hug had indeed comforted him.

But it had also aroused him and inspired him with confidence that he hadn't lost his touch after all.

She looked at her phone, at the door, then at Jason. "I guess I better go. Do you think he'll call me a cab?" She tilted her head toward Vinny at the other end of the bar.

"No need," he said. "I'm leaving, too. I'll give you a ride."

"You're so sweet. That'd be great."

* * *

And now here she was in his car, saying it again—"You're so sweet" —when he complimented her legs. Third time, he thought, is indeed the charm.

"So, where to?" he asked and tried to stop staring at those lovely, toned, smooth legs.

"Just home, I guess. I'll grab some leftovers and then maybe Mom'll be home and can drop me at Atomic."

He started the Audi and considered his next approach. He couldn't risk taking her home and having Mom show up to ruin the mood. And he couldn't offer to take to the Atomic later because he'd despise the music, not to mention that her friends might be there to distract her. He considered a dinner offer, somewhere quiet and dim. But she didn't really seem like a quiet and dim kind of girl.

"Home it, is," he said. "What's the address?" She told him. He backed out of his spot, and as he shifted into Drive, he said, "Hey, do you mind? My place is on the way. My back's acting up and I need a pill."

"Whatev'," she said cheerily. "It's okay with me."

He maneuvered the roads in such a manner that he hoped she wouldn't notice that his place was not exactly "on the way." She seemed not to. He asked questions about being an anchor woman, and she explained that jobs were, like, really hard to find and that the few she'd found always got filled by someone "with experience." "I mean, really," she huffed, "how hard can it be? I look great on camera—all my professors said so—and I keep up with *ET*, so I always know what the stories are. I could do it easy. I'd be great."

He agreed.

At his house, he unlocked the door and then stepped aside to let her enter first. As she passed through the doorway, he lay his hand against her side as if guiding her. "Can I get you something? A glass of wine, maybe?"

She shrugged. "Sure, I guess. As long as it's not that sour kind, you know. What do they call that?"

He guessed at her meaning. "Dry?"

"That's it, dry. I don't like that kind."

He kept his hand on her side and stepped up next to her other side, guiding her to the kitchen. "I'm sure I'll have something you'll like," he said and silently prayed that he still had that bottle of Chateau d'Yquem a grateful client had given him.

Mindi shrugged the long chain of her tiny purse—just wallet sized, really—off her shoulder and dropped the purse onto the long bar separating the kitchen from the dining room. She climbed into one of the tall bar chairs while he located the wine. "Your kitchen is great," she said and fingered the mesh of a wire basket full of onions and potatoes.

Jason uncorked the wine. "Thanks." He fancied himself a bit of a chef and so enjoyed the spacious kitchen, complete with a six-burner stove, a convection oven, and yards of granite counter top. He set a glass of wine in front of her. "See if that suits you." She sipped and nodded. Jason reached for a remote against the wall to his left, pressed a button, and Traffic's original version of "Feelin'Alright?" flooded the room. To his surprise, Mindi bobbed her head to the music and hummed along. "You know this song?"

She nodded. "When I was little, after my dad left, I spent a lot of time at my grammy and grandpa's. Grandpa played this old timey music all the time." She stopped talking to sing along when the chorus struck up: "Feelin' alright? I'm not meanin' to shoot myself."

"You know," Jason said, "the words are actually—" He stopped himself. No need to embarrass her. Better, he thought, stung by her second comparison of him to her grandpa, to correct that misconception. "You know, I'm not really your grandpa's age. But I heard a lot of this music growing up." Born in 1964 he had, indeed, grown up hearing and loving this music, and he had never acquired a taste for the big-hair bands or the Michael Jackson-Madonna-Cindy Lauper kind of sounds that might be considered closer to the music of his generation.

She either hadn't heard him or didn't care, for she made no response. "I'm going to get those pills," he said. "Be right back." He rounded the bar, crossed the dining room, and turned left down a hallway. In the bathroom he rattled a bottle of Advil and ran a little water, just for authenticity's sake. "Whole Lotta Love" cranked up as he walked back, and he thought perhaps he should switch to something softer, more romantic. On the other hand, he owned no contemporary pop music and she likely was not a fan of jazz or big band. At least this was familiar to her and might keep her feeling comfortable.

Back in the kitchen, he stood opposite her at the bar. She still bobbed her head to the music. "More wine?" he asked.

"Just a little. It's good." He poured. "Thanks. Hey, where's that bathroom? I gotta pee." Nothing shy about this girl, he thought. Another good sign. He pointed the way, and once he assumed she was safely ensconced, he headed down the same hallway, intending to click on a dim lamp by his bed and light the five candles on his dresser. But the bathroom door remained wide open, and when he instinctively looked in, there she sat.

"Whoa, sorry," he said and turned away.

She just giggled. "No prob, I'm covered."

He glanced back. Her little black skirt bunched around her waist and her little black panties puddled around her ankles, but the important parts were nevertheless out of sight—barely. "No offense," she said, "but not having a bathroom door is kind of weird."

Distracted by the view, he missed a few beats before registering what she had said. "Oh, no, no, there's a door. It's a pocket door."

Clearly tipsy, she giggled again. "A pocket door. What, do you, like, keep it in your pocket?"

"No. Well, sort of." He reached for the brass latch, popped it up, and pulled the door out a few inches. "It's here, in the pocket of the wall."

"Wow. Like magic. Like a secret panel or something. That's great."

He stifled a laugh because he'd be laughing at her, not with her. "Right. It saves space."

"Okay," she said, "I'm gonna finish up. You gonna keep watching?" Much as he wanted to, he said no and pulled the door to.

With no time now to light the candles while she was occupied, he walked back to the kitchen." She, too, returned and climbed up onto the her chair.

"More wine?" Tipsy was good, he thought. Not drunk, just tipsy.

"I shouldn't," she said. "I'm kinda feeling it, you know?"

"Sure," he said. "Okay."

"But maybe just a little." She grinned her bright white grin. He poured. Bob Dylan sang "Blowin' in the Wind," and again she hummed along and again she fingered the wire mesh basket. "The thing is," she said, "about this music, you know, a lot of it doesn't make much sense."

"I guess not," he agreed.

"I mean, like this song. I guess it's about nature and all that stuff, but I don't really get 'The ants are my friends, just blowin' in the wind'."

"No, it's—" he began but once again stopped himself. "I don't really get it either."

She moved her hand from the basket to its contents and began shuffling potatoes and onions as if she were after something. "I mean, I don't know, I guess ants are pretty light. Maybe they can blow in the wind. I've never seen one blow in the wind, but I guess it could happen. Do you think it could happen?"

He laughed and laid his hand against her cheek. "What I think, is that you are absolutely precious." He considered for a moment, then added, "You're great."

63

She smiled. "Hey, look. She fished a potato from the bottom of the basket and held it up in front of him. "*That's* great," she said.

He studied the misshapen potato. "It's a heart."

"Yeah," she beamed. She turned it over. "Or a butt. Or boobs." She giggled.

"Exactly," he said. "But nowhere near as beautiful as yours."

She straightened in her seat and pushed out her chest. "They are pretty great, aren't they?"

He nodded. "Better than great. They're perfect."

"Hey," she beamed, "wanna see something?" She slipped the top button of her blouse undone and pulled the blouse aside to reveal a significant portion of her right breast and the rim of her black bra. In the soft flesh of the lovely white breast, just outside the bra line, she sported a small, bright red heart tattoo. "Heart and boob, see? Like the potato."

He stared. "Much better than the potato."

"You are the sweetest," she said. "I've got one on my right butt cheek, too."

"I'd love to see it."

"It's just like this one. Right in the big fat middle of my butt cheek." She giggled almost uncontrollably.

He leaned onto the counter, his face just inches from hers. "Listen, why don't we kick off our shoes, put our feet up—" He nodded vaguely in the direction of his bedroom. "—and get to know each other."

"We know each other," she giggled. "You're Jason, I'm Mindi— remember, two *i*'s no *y*—and we both like Vinny's and you—" She stopped suddenly and looked in the vague direction he had indicated, then back to his face. "Wait, did you mean—" Her face scrunched and she blurted, "Eew!"

Jason visibly flinched. "Eew?"

"Sorry. No offense. It's just, you know, you're, like, old."

Eew. You're old. At least the previous two hadn't acted disgusted, just politely eased away before, he told himself, he had a chance to work his magic. Had they, too, thought *eew*?

"I'm sorry, Mindi. I didn't—"

She waved his words away. "No prob. You're not the first old guy to hit on me. But you are definitely the sweetest." She leaned in and kissed his cheek. "Really, you're great. But, you know."

She was truly precious. He'd been a fool, and a lecherous fool at that. "Yes, I know. Listen, you're a lovely girl with a tender heart." He grinned. "The real one, not the boob one."

She smiled back. "Hey, the boob one's pretty great."

"Yes," he said. "It's pretty great." He straightened. "So, I should take you home."

"I'll just grab a cab."

"No," he said.

"Yes," she said.

He relented. "Okay. But at least let me call."

He called, gave his address, said the driver should honk when he arrived. But he needn't have bothered with the last instruction because Mindi had already scooped up her tiny purse and headed toward the front door. He followed.

On the front porch, they stood in awkward silence until she said, "Really, it's okay. You're great."

"Not sure," he said. "But you are definitely great."

She stepped over to him, hugged him tightly, then stepped back. "Maybe we'll see each other. You know, at Vinny's or something."

"Maybe."

The cab arrived, and she was gone.

Back inside, he sat at the kitchen bar, staring down at the granite countertop. *Eew. You're old.* For the first time in his life, he knew it was true. He was old. Forty-seven. Almost fifty. He'd never heard of the Crabmasters, nor did he care. He knew the words to "Feelin' Alright?" and "Blowin' in the Wind." He owned a house with a pocket door.

Eew. You're old. God, he was twice her age. He'd struck out three times, and to top it off he'd lost his first sale ever. He was old. He'd lost his touch. He was done. He needed to reassess. And he needed a drink. But not here. Not alone. He needed movement. He needed noise. He needed distraction. He grabbed the heart-shaped potato she'd left on the counter and dropped it in the trash. He headed for Vinny's.

* * *

As he expected, business at Vinny's had grown since he'd been there earlier. He parked several rows out. As he approached the entrance, he smelled cigarette smoke, and when he stepped into the light at the door, a cloud of it wafted into to his face. He waved it away and detected a whiff of cloyingly sweet perfume as well.

"Sorry," a woman's voice said. He peered beyond the light where she stood in semi-darkness, the cigarette glowing between her fingers. "It's a bad habit, I know."

Despite his growing depression, the old habits kicked in. "No problem. I used to smoke," he said, although he'd never touched a cigarette in his life. "Still love the smell."

"You're probably lying," the voice said. "But you're sweet to say so."

You're sweet. It's what Mindi had said. "That perfume," he said, "that's what I like smelling."

She stepped into the light, crushed her cigarette out in the ashcan near the door. "Quite the charmer, aren't you?"

She appeared about his age and somehow familiar. Did he know her? Unlikely. He had dated only two women his age and those only briefly. But surely he'd remember if she were one of them. She wore tan slacks and a bright red pullover blouse, moderately vee-necked. Not spectacular, he thought, but not bad. He opened the door and motioned for her to go first.

"You're a gentleman," she said and bowed slightly before entering.

He spotted one empty stool at the bar and approached it. She followed. "Please," he said. "Help yourself." He motioned to the stool.

"Thanks. But I'm just getting a drink."

He sat. Vinny, drawing a beer for another customer, waved that he'd be there shortly. Jason studied the woman. A little thick in the middle, but not fat. Face, perhaps a bit puffy, but smooth and attractive. She had attempted to disguise slight bags under the eyes with make-up. And the eyes, bright, lively, and again somehow vaguely familiar.

"I'll be happy to buy your drink," he said.

"Thanks, but I'm with friends." She pointed a thumb over her shoulder to some table behind them. "My yoga group. We're celebrating a year together."

"Yoga. That's healthy. Congratulations."

Vinny arrived and took her order first. Gin and tonic." Good for her, she liked the taste of alcohol.

Vinny fetched the drink, and when he returned Jason said, "It's on me." The woman turned to him. "I know," he said, "the yoga group." But it's still on me."

She raised her glass. "Cheers."

"And to you."

"The usual?" Vinny asked, and that's when it struck Jason. The familiar look, the familiar eyes, the yoga group. "Wait," he said to the woman's back. She stopped, turned. "Are you by any chance related to someone named Mindi—two *i*'s, no *y*?"

The woman looked surprised. "You know Mindi?"

"We've met. Sweet girl."

"My daughter," she smiled. "Sweet, yes, but I wish she'd find a real job."

"Daughter? I would have guessed sister."

"You are a silver-tongued devil, aren't you?"

"I mean it. You're lovely."

She raised her glass once more. "And you, sir, are bullshit. But you're the best bullshit I've heard in a long time. To your health and happiness." She sipped the gin and tonic.

"Mindi said," he blurted before she could get away, "that you might be looking for a house." He slipped a business card out of his shirt pocket. "If you need anything, give me a call."

She read the card. "Thanks. I just might." She tucked the card down her vee-neck, presumably into her bra, then turned and walked to a table seating four other middle-aged women. Middle-aged, he thought. Not old.

He faced the bar. "Feelin' alright?" Vinny said.

He considered the question, nodded. "Not meanin' to shoot myself."

Thomas de la Cruz

Gallos

"Where's Daniel?"

The tip of my father's work boots pinned the back of my mother's sandals as he came up behind her.

"You're going to step on me, quítate."

"Where's Daniel te dije." I walked into the kitchen, and moved slowly towards him. He started to say something to my mother, but then closed his mouth and looked at me while breathing through his nose.

"I was playing hide-and-go-seek."

"Are you a girl, mijo?"

"What?"

"'Mande' se dice, and you don't look like a girl."

"Leave him alone, Octavio."

"Well if he's not a girl then why isn't he outside with the men? Huh?"

I looked at my mom who half smiled then back at my father. "I was playing hide—"

"You want to be in the kitchen with your mom? Like a girl? The kitchen is for women, mijo."

My mother quickly turned from chopping tomatoes, and slapped my father's stomach. "But you spend a lot of time eating here, verdad? Panzón." The loud smack resonated through the house.

"Didn't hurt." He turned and started walking towards the door, but stopped and pointed at me. "Come outside." He walked out without saying anything else.

Luis stood outside with my father and uncle, and I could tell instantly, by the hole he dug with the heal of his shoe, that he lamented having opted to hide outside. Luis' my uncle's only boy out of four children, and my best friend.

"Daniel," my father said while keeping his eyes on my uncle. "You're gonna fight Luis today."

I felt like laughing, but neither my father or uncle seemed to be joking, so I pointed gently at Luis. "But I don't want to fight him."

"You've never been in a fight, right?"

"No."

"Pos ay ta." How are you going to be a man?"

"But we're friends."

"¿Y qué? Me and your uncle fought all the time." ¿Verdad qué sí, José?"

My uncle tossed his head back as he smiled at him. "That's part of being a man. But we'd fight with sticks and terrones."

My father flicked my ear with his middle finger." "Hit me with a shovel once."

"You hit him with a shovel, Tío José?"

"It wasn't a shovel, it was a broom. Got him in the face. Chécale you can still see the mark."

I turned to my father, but the garage light only illuminated the thin strands of hair on his head.

"It was a shovel, te toy dejiendo." My father's response shook his arm and a little beer spilled from the can he held. "But I got you, too."

"Sí, but you were older."

"I still am older."

"Yeah, but it doesn't matter now. So wachale."

"Tampoco." Baja el pecho, o te lo bajo."

"Ha. I don't think so."

"You don't?"

"No I don't."

Very deliberately they both took a sip from their beers, but didn't stop staring at each other. They were about to take another sip, but my father lowered his can before it touched his lips. "No me mires con tantos huevos."

"I'll look at you how I want."

"You won't be able to if I close both your eyes, con unos jabs."

"Sí, hombre."

I turned to Luis who wore a thunder cats t-shirt that didn't protect him from the chilly night. With his hands in his pockets he half smiled at me.

"Ponte trucha, Daniel." My father's words caught me off guard, and I quickly turned to look at him. "Métele unos jabs a Luis," he ordered.

Why did he want me to fight Luis? If anyone picked on me at school it was okay to fight. He told me that constantly, but Luis and I were friends and he never picked on me. After a few moments of staring at me he crossed his arms, and locked his knees. His look of expectation changed to the look he gives me when I've done something wrong. Unblinking eyes, tongue in between his upper lip and teeth, nodding slowly then progressively faster. But I hadn't done anything wrong. I tried not looking down, but couldn't help it.

"¿Qué tienes?" my uncle said. "Luis is going to kick Daniel's ass. Verdad qué sí, mijo?" I saw Luis out of the corner of his eyes looking at me, but I kept my eyes on my father. My uncle stepped closer to him, and grabbed his skinny arm. "You're afraid of, Daniel?"

I knew he still stared at me, but I refused to acknowledge it. Instead I looked down and kicked a small rock at my feet. Finally he looked towards my uncle and said, "No, but—"

"¿Y tú, Daniel?" My father stepped closer to me and tapped me with his knuckles. "¿Le tienes miedo?"

I never considered if I feared Luis. Why would I? But Luis had said he wasn't afraid of me. What else was I supposed to say? A little louder than I expected I answered, "I'm not afraid of him."

"Daniel's not afraid of anyone?" My father stepped away from me.

My uncle jabbed the air and shouted. "¡Va a haber pedo! Sorry Daniel, but you're going to knockout city.

My father took a swig from his beer, and pointed at José. "Ha." Luis is going to roll up in a ball like you used to do. That's what's going to happen."

"¿Qué? You never knocked me out."

"No? What about the time we were at Frank's house? I got you con el right hook. Mocos y al piso. All rolled up in a little ball. Amá amá, Octavio hit me. ¡Amá!"

"I never cried to Mom, mentiroso."

"Yes you did."

"Nunca, nunca, nunca. Man you're such a liar."

The hand my father held the beer can with came to his side, and his back straightened out. "José. You're calling me a liar? Tú, a mí?"

My uncle threw back his head. "This again? Let it go."

"How many times? Huh? How many?"

"Bueno, ya hombre."

My father started towards José, but then turned to Luis and me. "Hombres don't cry to their dads when they get their ass kicked by their brothers, entienden."

My uncle put his beer can to his mouth, but didn't take a drink." "Same story, all the time, every day, same story."

"And is it a lie? Huh?"

"It was only once or twice that I told Apá."

"Estas bien idiota. He got me more than one or two times."

"He wouldn't even hit you hard?"

My father chucked his can at my uncle's feet and beer inside it shot out over his pants. After a few seconds of staring I felt like saying something, but any involvement on my part would only direct their anger towards me. Like when you're walking back from school and two dogs are growling at each other in the middle of the street. You can throw rocks at them from afar, but you really don't want to pass in between them.

"Alright güey," my uncle finally said. "But you were bigger than me y te estabas aprovechando. You would hit me real hard."

My father stared at him for a moment and then walked towards the ice chest." "You were a pain in the ass that's why," he said, while pulling out another beer. "And you still are. Some things don't change."

"I may still be a pain in the ass, but I'm not that little kid anymore."

"You're still a mocoso, and if Apá were here you'd cry to him again."

"Cry? ¿Porqué? You can't do nothing to me." My uncle began shadow boxing with the smoke coming from the pit. "Even the smoke goes down, mira."

My father tossed his head back. "Ha. I'll put you to sleep right next to the ice chest and you'll wake dreaming of—"

"Cállate la boca. I'll give you the first shot because that's the only one you're gonna get."

"Hermanito I only need one pa mandarte knock out city."

"Maybe if you hit me with a bat."

"Nope one. Just like when we were kids."

"You never knocked me out."

"No? Te *noquié* like Daniel is gonna knock out your son. Órale Daniel, échatelo."

My stomach tightened up and I looked away from my father's silhouette. Even in his state of inebriation my uncle caught my reaction. "Ya ves. Oh I don't want to fight." I want to be friends."

My father turned his whole body towards me. "Is that true, Daniel?"

It was true. I didn't want to fight Luis, but the way he asked made me feel ashamed to admit it. I looked at Luis who offered no support. What if he wants to fight me? He had already said he wasn't afraid. If I say I want to be friends then Luis will be free and I'll be the one who backed out. "Well if Luis want to…"

"Just like you, Octavio. Backing out." My uncle threw his arms into the air along with his beer.

"Hey shut up. Yo nunca me rajé de los jabs."

"Yeah, but you would only fight me. Remember la time you spoke to the Mormons, and I went to la quince to throw jabs with Flaco, Doiler y Sapo? Huh y esa time. Oh, I'm too busy talking to Mormons."

"They weren't Mormons."

"Who cares what they were it's the same thing."

"Now your memory sucks. They were Jehovah Witnesses."

"What's the difference?"

"Mormons believe in José Smith and Jehovah Witnesses don't."

"José Smith? Es Joseph Smith. Not José."

"Same thing. But I was talking to the Jehovah witnesses that day."

"So you remember. You backed out and I went solo to the mile fifteen."

"I told you to wait for me."

"Why were you talking to them anyways? Somos católicos."

"There was a pretty girl with them and I wanted to talk to her."

"¿Qué? So you pretended to listen so you could talk to her?"

"Pos, yeah." My uncle laughed until he started coughing but stopped when my father shoved him. "What are you laughing at?"

"You must be adopted, carnal."

"¿Porqué?"

"Get a load of your dad, Daniel. That's why I had more girls than him when we were in school." He leaned closer and placed his hand around his mouth. "And I got more girls than him today, too."

My uncle José has three daughters, but something about the way his tongue played with the side of his mouth told me that he wasn't talking about them. I looked at Luis who opened his mouth slightly, but then closed it and looked away. "More girls?" I finally asked.

"Sí mijo."

"Y tía Felipa?"

"What about her?" He leaned in closer and pulled Luis and me towards him. His beer can rested on top of Luis' shoulders. "Don't tell your moms eh, but I still get girls, mira." He reached into his back pocket and took out his wallet.

I looked to my dad who sipped his beer slowly. "You guys are little, but later you'll learn," he finally said, while swiping the carton of cigarettes from the top of my uncle's Tahoe.

"Mira." My uncle waved his hand in front of my face and directed my eyes to a piece of paper he held in his hands. "Numbers from all over the valley, mijo. Eh, como la ven. Your dad would have as many as me, but he doesn't know how to talk to them like I do."

I quickly turned to my father and forced my eyes to see his face. The garage light illuminated his glossing eyes, which looked at me briefly then turned away. He raised his chin. "I have enough. Don't worry."

I looked at my uncle who closed his eyes, smiled and started shaking his head. Then I looked back at my father. "Enough?" He lit his cigarette and then looked at me but kept quiet. He stared at me, took a drag of his cigarette, and blew the smoke into the air. He heard me I know he did. Enough? Enough what? He took another drag from his cigarette, and still remained silent.

My uncle stood up quickly and looked at my father. "You know how I do it? I go up to them like a man and say, 'hey mija. Tú y yo. Y es todo."

"That never works, mentiroso."

"Yes it does. That's how dad told me how to do it."

"Dad taught me how to do it before you were even born."

"Pos he taught me como hombre. Not like a vieja like you."

"¿Vieja? I wasn't the one crying every time I'd kick your ass."

"I never cried."

"You always cried. Like your son's gonna cry right now. Órale Daniel, échatelo."

Simultaneously both he and my uncle turned towards us. I felt three pairs of eyes on me, but the only ones I could stand looking back at were Luis'.

"Are you going to cry, Luis? Huh?" My uncle kicked up some caliche rocks towards him. "Are you a girl or you gonna fight like a man?" Luis looked at me, but I too waited for the answer. He looked back at my uncle for a few moments, and then glanced at my father until finally resting his eyes on me.

"Qué onda, Daniel? He's staring you down, mijo. He's waiting for you to do something."

I didn't know what my father saw in his eyes, but I saw fear and a yearning for me to get him out of the situation. He continued to look at me with those eyes. Look down, Luis. Run away. Stop standing there. Get us both out of this. Look down. Stop looking at me.

"Luis, don't let him look at you like that. Lift your chin up, mijo. Lift it up."

Luis' eyebrows began getting closer together and his lips tightened up. Slowly he lifted his chin and took his hands out of his pocket. My thumb and index finger started rubbing against each other, but I only noticed because my father pointed it out.

"Mira, he's anxious."

Anxious? I looked down at my hands and clenched my thumb and index fingers. When I looked up Luis still stared at me. What are you looking at? What is it? Stop staring at me. Why didn't you just stay inside the house? Finally one thought managed to break free, and in a strange voice I said. "What are you looking at?"

His chin came down slightly, but then went up higher. "What are you looking at?"

"Stop looking at me like that." I raised my right hand and pointed at him.

"I'll look at you like I want."

"You want to fight?"

"Do you?"

"If you want?"

My father came up to me and placed his hand on the lower part of my back. "Órale."

He shoved me towards Luis with enough force that my arms flailed behind me as I flew forward. Smack. I felt the palm of Luis' hand on my cheek, and his long fingers poked my right eye. I stumbled back and rubbed it with the back of my hand.

"Ha, that's what you get for trying to cheap shot, Daniel." My uncle held his beer can up and began bouncing. "Don't give him a chance, mijo. He's stunned."

Luis began moving towards me and I could hear my father's voice in the background shouting like he did when we'd take a rooster to Chuy's house. "Pegale Daniel, chingao."

Why had he hit me? My face was wide open, and he saw that I'd been pushed. He should've moved, but instead he hit me. I brought my right leg from behind me and found the inside of Luis' thigh. He screamed out in pain and slowly fell to the floor.

"Get up, mijo. Órale." I could see my uncle's face at Luis' ear, but his words competed with my father's.

"You got him, Daniel."

Luis tried getting up, but I put my knee on his chest. With my left hand I pushed his face into the light orange caliche. His arms flailed, so I brought down my fist onto his cheek bone. Smack. Why didn't you look away? Smack. You're not afraid of me? Smack. This is all your fault.

I don't remember hearing my father's voice after that, but I do remember Luis' cheek bone getting red and swollen and eventually popping like a tamarindo bag when you squeeze too hard. After a while both my eyes started tearing up and made it difficult to see.

"What are you two doing?" I got off of Luis immediately after hearing my mother's voice. Through the smoke and blinding tears I saw her practically stepping on my father's toes.

"They gotta become men, Flor."

She turned away from him as Tía Felipa lifted Luis off of the ground.

"Como se va ser hombre if you pick him up when he cries? Eh?"

"Men like you two? Pelados, es lo qué son. No hombres." My mother's chastising did nothing to hinder the joy in my father's eyes. She then turned to me. "And you?" I looked down and instantly started crying. Thick teardrops accumulated at the ends of my eyelashes and I couldn't see. "Let me see you." She placed her hands on my cheeks and brought up my head. "Vente." Let's go inside.

On the way inside I could hear my father shouting "Hey come on. Don't cry eh. You're a man, right?"

My mother sat me at the kitchen table, and with a wet towel began wiping my face. Tía Felipa turned red as she spoke about my uncle, and pressed a Ziploc bag filled with ice against Luis' cheek. I tried not to look towards him, but my mother's face only made me cry harder. Luis didn't look angry even with red eyes, busted cheek, mucus lips and graveled hair. We felt comfortable while sitting in the kitchen with our mothers. But, when they asked us what had happened, we still managed to blame each other.

Cheryl Clements

Host of Heaven

Vaginas don't interest her, so my student says, though she claims that obstetrics/gynecology is in her future. "I want to help make babies," she explains. "But the whole vag thing...." She draws a circle, one of considerable circumference, in the air and shakes her head. "Don't want to see it. Want nothing to do with it. I'll be a gyno, but I'm dodging that bullet."

On this the first day of fall semester 2013, I've asked my students to announce their career goals, to make them open up and feel at ease. How can I tell this bright-eyed, anatomy-impaired gal that when one has a job in gynecology, one can't dodge the vagina bullet? How can I tell her that the "vag" is not just the occupation's target but its bull's eye?

Instead, I ask her, "So what will you do when you're giving a physical exam? Call in a volunteer from the lobby to describe your patient's vagina for you?"

My ob/gyn has been my doc for eleven years, and later in the week when I see him for a six-month follow up—another exam to learn if he's still concerned there's a hitch in my plumbing's get-along—-I go into Dr. Davis's office with plans to recreate my student's vision of her future. Instead, we end up discussing other stories, the copies of my published work that I gave him last visit.

"I did read your essays," Dr. Davis says. "I laughed in some places, but some scenes were so dark." He paused as he examined my breasts and repeated, "Really dark. Why do you write such dark stuff?"

This isn't the first time I've been asked that question. In fact, my fellow English prof and trusted proofreader Lea Williamson once claimed that when she starts one of my pieces and laughs, she knows she'll pay for it later in the essay.

I could remind anyone who's perplexed that this combo of humor and sorrow isn't original to me. This past July, I was even advised to make more of it when my uncle and I visited with Skip Hollandsworth at a writer's conference. We'd heard Skip's talk on his film *Bernie*, a flick about an old woman who winds up murdered and stored in a deep freeze, and after his presentation, I suggested that perhaps Skip might have an interest in another such crime—one that would be double the fun as it resulted in not just one but two old women dead. No one on ice, though.

As we stood among other conference attendees in the hotel lobby, Skip's head was without adornment. However, I could see from his shift in posture—shoulders back, jaw set, and arms crossed—that at my mention of a story idea, he'd just donned his editor's hat. "No. It needs something more than just a murder."

"More? Like what?"

"Like something to make it more than just a murder."

"I see." I considered this. "It needs a refrigerator?"

He nodded. "That's right. It needs a refrigerator."

I shared this wisdom with my Uncle Lee during our four and a half-hour drive from Grapevine to College Station later that afternoon. It should have been a three-hour tour, but my uncle—who's traveled with my husband, John, and me throughout Great Britain—has grown to accept that when I'm behind the wheel, we'll be lost almost as often as found. My uncle doesn't mind the delay but gets annoyed when I don't despair that we're on the wrong path and that I sometimes even slow down to admire the scenery. Lemonade out of lemons, I always say, and my refusal to fret pisses him off, as usual.

As I lie on the examination table, I consider telling Dr. Davis that he's not alone in being perplexed by my odd humor, by my alternating between light-hearted and dark or between virtue and evil. I consider letting him know that the contrast is one of the ways I'm a mystery, but when he moves to the end of the table to begin his pelvic exam, I decide I'm in no position to tell Dr. Davis anything of the sort. No mystery here. At this moment, I'm an open book.

After the exam and review of my most recent blood work, Dr. Davis tells me the safest move, a sure-fire remedy, is to clean house. I need a hysterectomy. This Christmas break is a good time, and he adds me to his schedule. Understand, there's no family medical history to suggest I might be in for trouble—because I've no family medical history at all. Without any knowledge from either my biological mother or father, Dr. Davis has no clue what genetic hand I've been dealt. So rather than risk playing out a bad hand, he suggests we just take the cards off the table.

"If you're not planning to have more children," he says, "your uterus is just . . . weight."

In his pause between "just" and "weight," I hear the unspoken, the word "dead."

Once home that day, I sit down to dinner with John and our only child—our ten-year-old daughter, Marlene—and decide to share Dr. Davis's verdict with my husband after I've had more time to digest it alone. This surgery is a familiar one to me. My stepmother had a hysterectomy about fifteen years ago. The surgeon at M.D. Anderson told her the tumor was easy enough to remove—just like picking up a suitcase, her doc reported. Everything was contained and neatly packed. Just like a good suitcase.

After John and Marlene head to bed, I stay downstairs and turn on the television. I settle on one of the channels my husband can't stand, a network that gives all its airtime to profiling true and tried murderers. The story featured tonight, I decide, isn't worth my time—dead folks galore but no refrigerator in sight, and I click off the TV. About midnight I end up opening the door to my own frig, take out a carton of lemonade, pour a glass, and add two shots of vodka.

I'm just getting settled onto the couch again in the dark living room of our dark house when Marlene comes down the stairs. I ask her if my moving about in the kitchen has awakened her, and without waiting for her answer, I apologize. But she says that's not the problem. The problem is the full moon. It's coming through the blinds in her bedroom.

"Haven't you noticed it, too?" she asks.

I told her long ago that she'd inherited her inability to sleep on a bright night from me, but I hadn't even noticed until now that the room has a low-grade glow. She joins me on the couch, and I cover her with my sweater.

As she closes her eyes but keeps talking—Marlene has more news to share from her school day—I lean back and peek out the curtain to see our backyard, which borders the Brazos River, our closest neighbor. I admit that I'm not paying attention as my baby chatters. My thoughts are on how Dr. Davis needs to get on with his work and remove that suitcase I'm toting around for no good reason. I've no need for it. I've no need for it because I've no intention of going anywhere.

After all, why would anyone want to be anywhere but here, here where the moon is made beautiful by the dark—where the moon casts its line into the black Brazos and shines its liquid spender onto the grass?

Marilyn Robitaille

Sicily, Sicily, Sicily

It was one blissful afternoon
That we spent sipping wine
Opening our souls to Sicily
A sky as azure as the sea with ancient depths
Subterranean Phoenicians and their art
All around us in every measured breath

We drank in all that was Sicilian
Marsala churches, old men on motorbikes
Gleaming fish in markets, jazz at 2:00 a.m
Hotels crisply serviced with rose rooms
And old stone floors that whispered grief and love

We tethered to our Texas roots, but gave way easily
To fresh squeezed oranges and wicked sweets
All before 10:00 a.m. and real sobriety
That only came at times when dreams dispelled
Not likely with mountain ghosts and fog
Both well turned to narrow streets beyond us

We met the mayor and Michelangelo
All in a day's work of buses and ricotta cheese
Our safari travels led us to remote places
Magic made in painted tiles and olive oil
Midnight light shone through the silver trees
To guide us to our prayers and on our way

We walked through villages to one grand party
Pizza oven-fired with friendship full refined
We danced and found the beat in centuries
Long gone before us in the cadence
It didn't matter that no one spoke Italian
Because smiles spoke every bay-leaf syllable

Praise the old-templed gods for calling us
We were of an island for a time and knew the kin
In our bones we felt the sea and smelled the salt
Tasted all that came to us and said it in our dreams
Sicily, Sicily, Sicily

Let's Suppose You Know

Let's suppose you know
That I look into the deep pools of your eyes
And I see Africa. Sun deep in red sand. Hot.
You, longing for ebony, for history, for her history
But you pass by, longing still in the moonlight
Listening to lions pass in the bush. Knowing them
In their full flavor, a danger so complete you
Know sublime and close your eyes against
The siren call. In your tent on the savannah
Alone, the die cast for your fate without her.

Let's suppose you know
That in my dreams you call to me
Walking in the sand, you stop and smell the surf
Take count of boats on far horizon. The day is
Full of promise. Cloudless azure sky in full color.
Murmurs on the breeze. French phrases in the air.
Our cottage perched on a precipice full view
Napoleon's ramparts of a time, relentless waves
I watch you walking up the path through bougainvillea
Framed in pink blossoms, rich like spun sugar
Coming in our doorway, you bring the mystic
Mist. Sage. Lavender. A hint of musk.
You take my hand and kiss it
Gently, your breath against my skin
This is like Virginia's drowning
Without the rocks in pockets
Without the lovely water

Of a Moment Wild on Port Aransas Beach

Port Aransas beach where the living was not so easy
Washed out jeans and old cars, too much beer and
No satisfaction for the trouble
We found our way there with an ice chest and wild ones
Too untamed to notice that we had class and a dark blue Superbee
Cool and lots of horsepower under our hood, bolted up against
Stoned hooligans, one word mine, one word my mother's
Who thought we were on a mission trip to save sad souls
We were, I guess, but not to pray or lead the youth away from sin
We were inequities blessed with good highs and a fast car and funds
We booked a room in a hotel dump, forego the tent and sand fleas
Life is hard, but for good kids gone bad, not so much
The hotel smelled like dull sweat, but we were of the moment
Knowing this was our time of sordid pleasure.
Breathing in. Breathing out.
We paid the fee for that twenty-five cent mattress massage.
Then we merged with the mob on Port Aransas beach.
We plumped the air mattress, lay among the bad boys, and drank beer
More beer than humans should consume under a summer sun on a hot
        beach
We were of a moment wild, gone all bad to a dark place
Where love was on the radio, and we kissed long and hard
Bleached from sun, we slept like dead beached whales
All encompassed by the waves, by the bad boys, by the beer
I awakened to the end of the world, hot flames bearing down
Swollen brain, heavy, dull-lidded and befuddled, one lost soul
Crawl on hands and knees in forced supplication to the toilet god
And wish that I was dead, skin red and burning.
Where, I wondered, was the glamour?

Julie Chappell

Execution

The rattlesnake's head separated cleanly
for his sins—
he had dead eyes
and a forked tongue
and slithered
and lay in the path of *rightwisnesse.*

At 3, I only knew
the swift flash
of my mother's hoe
as she brought down
her justice
to that which lay in *our* way

to the garden.

Dogankhamun

Old dog lying in an afternoon sun
so hot it would boil tar

perhaps she senses this
as she moves to
shaded, cool grass
and to another spot
until inspired by
Akhenaten's holy disk
she trots away
back into the sun
to sniff
to defecate
to run with aged legs
for a moment made young again
in that Amarna-like sun.

Alcatraz

At 8, I watch my father, returned
from taking prisoners to Alcatraz,
bringing me a rock plucked from the Rock,
this rock, bearing life
rather than taking it.

A creature had attached itself
firmly onto the rock's surface
its shell unbroken
in spite of the long trip
from California to Kansas.

I didn't know from sea creatures
so I filled the bathroom sink
with water from the tap
plunged the rock into my sea,
the poor creature yet unseen
clinging for life
in that cold, fresh water,
emerging now
Venus on her half-shell
the sea snail awaking
from its confinement on the Rock.

At 42, I moved slowly
deliberately with the crowd
tuned to the audio tour as we walked
along the line of cells on Alcatraz
empty now save for echoes
of the Seven Deadly Sins
of every Commandment broken
of every social contract ignored
on both sides of the prison walls.

I thought of my little rock, that shelled creature
and my dad duty-bound to deliver
three, four, five, six men
shackled, chained from waist to ankles,

watching the scenery
from the windows of the vehicle
in which my father carried them
to their exile
tangible life slipping by
helped along by self-fulfilling prophecies
of a society contrived, unnatural against
poverty, color, and perversion

as the men shared with my father
the journey to this Rock
on which I now moved
years later through the same spaces
my father and his prisoners
had shared, if only for a little while,
all of us listening
time consumed by the sounds
of Alcatraz
cell doors clanging shut,
chained legs moving laboriously,
human voices stifled by confinement
by "99 years to Life."

A cruel irony
in confinement
on the Rock

as it floats on a cerulean sea
sparkling like the City
whose presence mocked those who watched
its wealth
its whiteness
its perversion
from the Rock

atop a shifting plate of rock
ready to shake them all free
into that shark-infested Bay
together.

Jerry Craven

Stone Salvation Barn

In the East Texas backwoods where three people could rightly be accused of being a crowd, Jack Tenner counted four buggies, five horses, and a mule, all standing close to the porch, and judging from the dust cloud up the road, there were more folk coming. Churchly folk, Jack reckoned, followers of that tent revival man who had set up his operation over in Woodville to pluck sinners right out of the deep woods and save them, sinners who liked the preacher man's brand of rant, Jack liked saying, sinners who dropped enough half dimes and pennies in the collection plate to buy the preacher-man a new buggy.

One of the buggies close to the porch looked to be new, so Jack figured the preacher himself stood behind Georgian and Jep Stone's house where he could gape at the barn. Maybe the preacher's wife came to make another drawing so she could take it to Jack's boss for another printing in *The Jasper News-Boy*.

None of the crowd was visible because of the abundance of undergrowth among the pine, oak, sweet gum, and magnolia trees around the house, especially the thicket that stood out back between the house and the barn. Georgian worked in front of his home, his tight straw hat jammed down to make his ears fold over like an angry cat. The idea of Georgian as a flickering-eared and foul-tempered cat made Jack chuckle. The cat-man had a pipe clamped between his teeth, one that gave off no smoke, and he worked in the final stages of hitching horses to his buckboard.

"Georgian," Jack said.

The man never seemed to look his way. "Jack."

"Seems like you got a passel of company."

"Ain't none of them welcome."

Jep stepped out the front door onto the abundant porch. "Jack," she said.

"Jeptha." Jack felt his heart beat faster. He tried not to stare at her tight cotton dress, a pink one that might have been red once, or at her blond hair that fell in ringlets past her shoulders, some tresses dangling over her breasts.

"You seen that bunch of pig-snouted, God-cursed nasty trash folk tromping around out back like a bunch of buzzard-kissing crap eaters looking for a fresh pile of manure?"

Her voice carried so much venom that Jack thought it best to hunker down. He dismounted, held the reins close in case Jep scared him so much he took a sudden notion to jump back on his roan and skedaddle. "Just got here. Ain't seen nobody but y'all."

"Theys out back, stomping down my okra."

"And the corn," Georgian said. "You wouldn't believe what those crude backwoods redbones be doing to my corn, and they claim to come in the name of God."

"They let your cattle loose?" Jack asked.

"Nope," Jep said. "But then we ain't got many."

"There's land owners around here," Jack said, "that would run them trespassers off with raising an angry voice and a shotgun, maybe firing some bird or rock salt their direction."

"I'd kiss them that done that," Jep said.

"Raising a gun ain't my style," Georgian said.

"Then it should be, and you know it. You ought to man up and blast away with my daddy's shotgun at that riff-raff."

Jack again winced at the poison in Jep's tone, though Georgian seemed to take no notice of it.

"My boss at the newspaper wants me to look at your barn," Jack said. "That okay with you?"

Georgian waved his hand almost in defeat. "Keep clear of the corn."

"And the okra. For sure stay out of my okra."

"I'm heading into Jasper for some supplies and for a talk with mister Kellie about what he prints in that newspaper of his." Georgian climbed into the buckboard.

"Would you like me take you to the barn?" Jep asked

Some years back, Jack thought, an invite from Jep to go to a barn with her would be one he would say yes to even if such a trip could be dangerous and foolish. He watched her finger a golden curl of hair on her breast. Even today, he thought, I'll sure as hell go with her, though the invite don't mean what a woman's invite to a barn ought to mean. But five years back, he remembered, when she took a fellow to a barn for the right reasons, it weren't me she took. It was Georgian Stone.

"Coffee," Jep said. "Last trip into town you forgot coffee, and don't you dare forget this time, or your ass is grass." She turned to Jack. "I'll tell you about Zarah and Reverend LeRoy Patterson on our way to the barn."

Jep said the preacher and his wife booked steamboat passage on the Laura from Beaumont. When they seen the barn, Jep told Jack, they went plum crazy, to hear Captain Andrew Smyth's account of it. "But before I tell much more," Jep said, "lemme explain about the paint."

She led Jack beyond the house, past the corn crib, through a patch of tobacco and into a stand of woods close to the river. "Last year," Jep said, "my garden proved a considerable producer. Watermelons. Squash. Sweetest tomatoes ever, and fine okra. Fine. That garden would have another good crop this year except for the preacher man's skunk stupid sinners hoofing around in it—all so they can gasp and raise their hands and speak idiotic noise to sound like talking but ain't. Stomped the onions flat, and most of the peas. Worst damage was to my okra. I got half a notion to take some pot shots at them while Georgian ain't here to know, and may God curse him for being no real man at all."

But her husband proved himself right smart at building, Jep admitted, something she admired in him from the first, even if he was a weird pacifist who refused to own a gun. "And who can live in these woods without no gun?" she demanded of Jack. "Least he don't complain none that I sometimes tote my daddy's shotgun."

Such scorn for her husband, Jack thought, ain't right. Still, he liked it that she and Georgian were's as cozy as they were back when she chose him over Jack.

Georgian's latest project, Jep said, "one to please me, which it ain't done, was a barn he built from the very cedar he cut down beside the river to make a place for the barn. Andrew Smyth had his boys tie them cedar logs into rafts, and he used that steamboat the Laura to shove them down river to the sawmills, along with hundreds of other logs, then he brought back first-class sawed boards to Bevilport, which Georgian hauled here to make the barn, though he claimed the boards like as not come from other logs and not the ones he cut. He's wrong, of course, I know, cause I recognized the color of the wood as being from our trees."

"The paint," Jack reminded her. He feared he sounded right irritated by her liking to talk a bunch, same irritated as he used to get back when she was a bit sweet on him, before Georgian landed in Bevilport, new to East Texas.

They picked their way around a couple of huge ant hills and a healthy patch of poison ivy on the grown-over logging road cutting through the forest toward the river. "Yeah." Jep shot him a mean look, no doubt, Jack thought, a warning not to interfere with her telling the story."

That barn, she said, was a thing of beauty, and she wanted Georgian to paint it special. "But did he get special paint? Hell no. He come home with nothing but whitewash, something he said would be good for the boards and might help the barn stay cool on hot summer days."

Then at least trim it in red, she told Georgian, to make it look like a proper barn.

"And he done it. He painted that barn white, then went to trimming the eves in the prettiest red you ever seen. I warned him to stop when clouds rolled up in the south, but did he stop? Not that stubborn man. He tried to beat the rain, which proved a fool's errand, and the rain came in a gully washer, set in like it wanted to rain forty days and forty nights."

When it dried up enough to inspect the damage, they found one side of the barn jagged and streaky with colors, red and pink, and some splotches the color of sun-burnt skin. "That day the rain made the paint run? That's the day when they seen it."

"Who seen it?" Jack paused at the edge of the woods, looked across the vegetable garden at the barn. "Looks good to me," he ventured.

"No it don't, and don't you say otherwise," Jep snapped. "Besides, they seen it from the river, remember, on account of being on that steamboat. They seen the other side of the barn, where the fresh red paint did all the running across the white, mixing with it, and making a real mess. Look at that pack of jackasses over there on the river side. My okra is on that side, and that's the side where they say God miracled a likeness of Jesus on that barn."

Jack tried for a straight face when listening to the Reverend LeRoy Patterson describe the barn. The woman Jack figured had to be Zarah Patterson sat nearby, her hand busy over a sheet of drawing paper, while the Reverend LeRoy held court with members of his flock of now-saved backwoods sinners: "The thorns, there, see them? That's what first caught Zarah's attention from way out there on the river, aboard the Laura. The crown of thorns and the blood, and there, the suffering face of Jesus—"

"I see it, Lord I see it," one of the men cried out.

"I believe, I believe. I do," a female voice said.

"—put there by the grace of God the Father on this miracle barn to remind us of His Son's sacrifice. He painted a blessed portrait of his son right here on Georgian Stone's building to make this a salvation barn."

"I don't see it," Jack said, not intending his observation to be an announcement, but it came out loud enough to get the attention of the preacher.

He strode over to Jack, leaving his little group waving their hands and murmuring. "Then let me show you. He's there, clear as day, his suffering face, his bloody tears." LeRoy took Jack's arm.

Jack pulled away. "Grab me like that again," Jack stifled a laugh, "and I'll poke you in the eye."

"Nothing can blind me to the presence of the Lord. Don't you see it there, the face covering most of the side of the barn? There, the thorns, there, the blood."

"If I hold my tongue just right and squint a bunch, and lean over this way," Jack leaned, tilted his head." "Then I see, lord I see. A barn with red and white paint streaked on it. And nope. No crown, no blood, no Jesus."

"Let me be your eyes," LeRoy said. "Better yet, let Zarah Grace Patterson be your eyes. Look, man, look at her drawing."

On the way back to his horse, Jep astounded Jack by taking his arm. "Seems like I made a mistake a few years ago," she said. "Georgian Stone ain't the man I took him to be."

Jack felt his pulse quicken but said nothing.

"You ought to come on in and sit a spell with me, now that Georgian has gone to town."

"Is that a wise idea?"

"Probably not. But I'd sure as hell like to spend some time with a real man, for a change. Seems like my living with Georgian is making me into someone I don't much like, sometimes."

When Jack got on his horse, Jep said, "I do wish you could come up with a way to keep them crazy redbones from stomping my garden flat there around my barn." Then she dropped her voice to a whisper, one Jack heard loud and clear: "There'll be another time for you and me, and I pray it's soon."

In the newspaper office Jack told his boss the new drawing he saw Zarah Patterson working on had more details than the one Kellie published in the *Jasper News-Boy*."

"Maybe I'll print it, too," Kellie said.

"I told the preacher-man I had to get back to report to the editor of the paper in Jasper," Jack said. "Which were a mistake. It made him double up his efforts to get me to see what he claimed to see, and he kept clutching my arm, jerking me this way and that with a wild look in his eye and a shrill edge to his voice so some of the redbones in his flock started giving me evil glances, maybe like they meant to do to me what they done to Jep's okra, which was for a fact stomped into the dirt." Jack didn't mention how sorry he felt for Jep standing all alone at the edge of her garden while he talked to the preacher-man. She looked like an abandoned child, which seemed fitting, given that her man was no man at all for doing nothing but heading to town to argue about what got published in the newspaper.

"You did a good job today," Kellie said. "As did I."

He seemed a bit full of himself, Jack thought, though he liked Kellie and would never criticize him to anyone. Still, Kellie's telling of his confrontation that day with Georgian Stone seemed to make the newspaper man puff up a bit more than usual.

Georgian had stomped into the newspaper office demanding that Kellie print a retraction to the story about Jesus on the barn. Never claimed it was true, Kellie said again and again until he tired of the tiff and told Georgian to leave. "But not before pointing to our motto hanging there on the wall," Kellie told Jack, and later told the same tale again and again to any around town who would listen.

In Jack's view it was a good motto, especially in the case of all the problems with the barn:

We Bend our Knee to None But God

The next *Jasper News-Boy* reported on the barn as well as on how curious folk had tromped down Jeptha Stone's garden, a note that pleased Jack. Kellie made no mention of Georgian in his article, though he did report that there was some open talk in town of burning the barn, rumors "this reporter" had heard in person, "rumors repeated by folk who took a dim view of witchcraft and any claims of magic because such unnatural happenings were always born of Satan and not the Lord, so—the rumormongers like repeating—the deep woods false temple with an idol on the side needed to have a torch set to it. Malicious rumors and such rogue calls for dastardly destruction of property," Kellie concluded in his news story, "are ones that everyone in the county as well as the whole state of Texas should heed, for burning a family's barn is serious business, there never being a good enough excuse for such malevolent action."

The only one in town, as far as Jack could tell, who spoke the rumors Kellie reported was the barber, a man with a loose tongue, in Jack's opinion. The barber seemed to take delight in declaring that somebody was going to get laid in the ground because of that barn.

Shotguns, the barber said, and Jack had listened to him mouthing off in the middle of his comical flurry of clacking the scissors in the pointless way he did between actually using them to snip hair. Buck shot, he said, like East Texas boys took with them to shoot the Yankees. Folks get het up over notions of religion, the barber said, and they can go to shooting each other for what looks like nothing, killing over the likes of that barn even, which somebody ought to burn before the madness rises so much that death jumps out of the barrels of guns right in the streets of Jasper, and never mind the barn sits nine miles out, down by the Angelina.

Such talk seemed silly to Jack, so he discounted any threats to Jep's barn.

But the Reverend LeRoy Patterson took them as real threats after he read the paper. He showed up outside the post office where he preached a sermon to passersby outside about how it was every God-fearing man's duty to protect the scene of "the second crucifixion that God painted on the side of Georgian Stone's barn."

Jack got to the post office for the last part of the sermon, the part where LeRoy promised to place armed guards by that barn until the threat by the forces of Satan abated. Jack figured the only threat to Jep's place wasn't barn burning but loony folk—the preacher's guards as well as sight-seers—tramping down what was left of Jep's garden.

When Kellie heard about the preacher's plan, he declared Jack needed to camp out on the river by the barn to watch what transpires. "But going could be dangerous, so you have the choice to stay away. If you do go, take no arms, and in no way get involved in anything people do out there. The moon's nearly full, so you should find watching the preacher man and his troop easy to do for most of the night."

The assignment from Kellie made going easier, though Jack had already decided to spend at least one night by that barn, given that Georgian wasn't man enough to stand up for Jep. There was no way Jack would go unarmed, though he figured his shovel would be a better weapon than his shotgun. Besides, gunplay struck him as an immoral solution to any problem.

What worried him more than a gun fight was the current in the river, a swift flow from recent rains. He knew he had one chance to dock his skiff close to the barn. If he missed, the current would push him considerably down river, so he would have to hike back through the thicket, something he wanted to avoid because of ticks. For sure there was no way he could row against the current if he overshot the area of the barn.

When Jack nosed his skiff to the bank near the barn and hopped ashore with the bow rope, he congratulated himself and his good fortune with the river. Five men were already there, four of them unloading camping gear from a raft staked to the bank. Jep stood on the rise above them, her arms akimbo and her face pinched into fury. Beside her the Reverend LeRoy Patterson waved his arms and hacked the air with his fists.

"...public property," LeRoy was saying, "and always has been. Fifty feet from any waterway, a hundred, and no matter who owns the land, people running a river have the right to come ashore to camp or for any reason they please."

"I think that ain't true." Jep turned to Jack. "And just what are you doing here?"

"Newspaper business. I'm here only to watch what folk do."

"You're welcome here," Jep said in a softer voice, "or to spend the night in our home, if you take a notion. But you other men, you ain't welcome nowhere around here. I got neighbors who say they just might up and shoot them that trespasses on my land."

"Dad burn it woman," LeRoy said. "We're here to protect this sacred barn because of having the exact likeness of Jesus painted right there, done by the hand of God himself."

"Don't say you ain't been warned. And you, Jack Tenner, you lay low if you hear shooting." She turned in a curt swirl of blond tresses and headed toward her house.

"Exact likeness," Jack muttered himself. "Exact." He took his bedroll from the boat, along with a can of beans and small tarp which he intended to sleep on. But he left the shovel out of sight in the skiff.

By the time darkness settled in and the four followers of the Reverend LeRoy built a fire from driftwood, Jack had spread his tarp a respectable distance from the saved sinners and the preacher man. He had also located a couple of huge ant hills like the ones that must have inspired the Smyths to name their place *Ant Hill Farm*. Mostly Jack stayed away from the Churchly crew, though after the sun set and the moon climbed among the tree tops, he wandered near the fire and asked LeRoy how he knew what Jesus looked like.

"Everybody knows that," LeRoy said. "Long hair, kindly face, trimmed beard, and eyes that can look into your very soul. You've seen paintings of Him hanging in most every church."

"All painted hundreds of years after he died—"

"And was resurrected."

"Okay, okay. Hundreds of years, and now nearly two thousand. So nobody knows what he looked like. That smudge you see on the barn ain't his exact likeness cause nobody knows it."

"The crown of thorns gives it away. Besides, God would not let people believe the paintings to be a likeness, not for two thousand years, unless it was true."

"Believing it makes it true." Jack spoke in a mocking tone.

"Yes. You speak wise words, my son."

"Anyone ever tell you that you're down right comical?" Jack went to his bedroll without waiting for a response.

Later in the night, after the campfire died to a glow of embers and several of LeRoy's flock filled the air with snoring, Jack retrieved the shovel from his skiff. He carried several shovels full of dirt from ant hills to spread beside each of Reverend LeRoy Patterson's saved sinners. The sleeping preacher-man got extra shovels of ant hill dirt.

The ants took longer than Jack expected to work their way into the clothes of the men, though when they finally climbed into place, they seemed to coordinate an attack of stinging. One man yelled, then another, then another. Jack watched them: dancing white shadows in the moonlight, figures slapping themselves, some using curse words that Jack was fairly certain were inappropriate for the newly saved. Perhaps it was the Reverend LeRoy Patterson who first shouted, "ants, ants." Those words were trigger enough for the lot of them to run for the river.

Jack counted the splashes, five of them, and he went to the water's edge to watch their bobbing heads whisked down river by the swift current.

Behind him a voice said, "I watched all that." Jep stood at the edge of her garden, holding a stick. "Like as not you saved them redbones in a more real way than any preacher-man ever did."

That's no stick, Jack thought: Jep came armed with a shotgun.

"You suppose any of them drowned?" Jep asked.

"Nah. Them deep woods redbones can all swim like water rats." Jack climbed the bank to get a closer look at Jep. He thought her mighty pretty in the moonlight, though there was something about her demeanor that disturbed him.

"So all they get is ant-stung and wet." Jep sighed. "That makes them lucky, for I came to do them some real damage. But now, just thinking how close I come to doing it, I got the shakes. Oh, Jack, you saved me from doing something terrible tonight."

"The shells in your gun. Loaded with bird or salt, right?"

"Buck. I weren't in no mood to be nice."

"Buckshot," Jack whispered. Damn. He stepped back. "You're kidding me. Tell me you're kidding."

"See for yourself." She broke open the shotgun, took out a shell, and stepped close to Jack. "Here," she jammed the shell into his shirt pocket. "Them men got lucky on account of you. I got lucky on account of you."

"Does Georgian know you came out here in the night to shed some blood?" Jack backed away, heading for his skiff.

"Maybe. Maybe not—and I don't care what he thinks. Where you going now?"

"I'm leaving."

"Will you come spend the rest of the night with me in the barn? Please? I need your company real bad right now, considering what I nearly done here tonight."

"The barn?" Jack stopped, looked at the barn. "I'll be damned."

He untied the skiff, stepped into it, and let the current take the boat.

Published in *descant 2013* and winner of the Frank O'Connor Award

TACWT 2013 Student Award Winners

Skyler Williams

Lamar University—Undergraduate Poetry Award
Grandfather's Boat & Other Poems

Grandfather's Boat (Wake of Colleen)

The bellow of her Buick 8
scattered egrets and redfish upon ignition
like soap dropped in a greasy skillet.
An ingenious amalgam of junk-yard scraps,
spare parts from the Gulfway machine shop—
she wasn't pretty but, damn, could she sing!
Her wooden hull's raucous vibrato
shattered the Sabine's brackish mirror,
earning stares from spiteful fisherman ready to
blame the day's small catch on *Colleen*.

Lover's Quarrel

Claws came out and we tore into each other's
faults, rending self-worth from bone with hateful haste.
Our first fight may have been vicious,
but the make-up sex was *animalistic*.

Our bodies growled spiteful words
in wet whispers, rhythmic echoes
of the passionate indictments we had
just apologized for.
I'll show you sorry, said
each thrust
each fresh bruise
each bead of sweat
each kiss.

Our muscles weren't chiseled
as sharply as our tongues,
but they all were working
hard.

Balloon at an Infant's Funeral

Heads bowed in prayer,
the room sits motionless
save the swelling of tears
and a single suspended balloon.
Discordant in its lightness,
tied to the handle of a casket
whose small dimensions
defy its sorrowful heft,
it rotates under dim lighting.
A macabre marquee of tinny silver
and pastel blue,
its silent cacophony
heralding *"Baby Boy!"*
in vibrant letters
as it pulls taut its silken tether.

Killer Deer Jerky

An obese man in a wheelchair sits alongside
a busy highway, prime real estate for refinery workers
hungry at shift's end. As carcinogens billow behind him,
he hawks strips of dried venison from coolers in the
bed of his truck, mimicking pioneers like Kraft and
Oscar Mayer.

Who knows? This man, in time, could be driving around
our great land in a car shaped like a rabid Bambi,
an old Grand Marquis with antlers so tall, routes will be
planned around low bridges. Our grandkids may enjoy
convenient, squeezable bottles of Killer Deer Jerky
brand meat product in containers designed to fit
the cup holders of their electric cars.

For now, he sits under his canopy,
building his tarpaulin empire one Ziploc bag at a time.

Barry Maxwell

Austin College—Undergraduate Nonfiction Award

Easy Journey to Other Planets

Five winters ago, Carter MacLaine's older cousin hog-tied him—trussed him wrist-to-ankle behind his back, and slammed him into the trunk of the family car. He drove to the dark roads beyond the glare of the city, beat Carter with fists and a tire tool, and left him.

After his cousin, his blood kin, drove away, Carter struggled back to the lighted places and survived. His body was broken, but not fatally. He was damaged, and permanently altered, but he lived.

I've never tried to extract any more details from Carter—there are layers of calamity he hasn't unbandaged, and a beating like his doesn't come from nowhere, after all. But his secrets are his to keep. If he decides to tell me more, he will.

Carter's life snapped that night like a brittle bone, and the fragments have been slow to knit. That he didn't die is what counts, and I'm glad of it, because Carter MacLaine is my friend.

We met like most friends do, at a lucky intersection of time, accident, and geography.

I had suffered a beating, too, but mine was self-inflicted. A harsh cocktail of pride, guilt, and shame had left me homeless and hung-over, as poor in cash as I was existentially penniless. Help from family was out of the question—I hadn't seen them in years, and the collateral damage from decades of heavy drinking had exhausted the sympathy and goodwill of any lingering friends. As a refuge of last resort, I took loose root in the ground of Austin's overburdened homeless shelter, on the books as client number 113-119.

The shelter was packed the morning Carter and I met, as it always is when the temperature drops, and in spite of months in and out the doors, I never felt part of the tribe. I'd come back from the men's room to find my scavenged copy of *The Accidental Tourist* had "got disappeared" from my chair, where I left it to mark my place. I'd closed my eyes and rested too long behind the locked restroom door, insulated from the roar of the lobby, ignoring the filth and the smell for the sake of the calm. Someone pounded for their turn and shattered the quiet, and meanwhile, a literate thief had liberated my book. I was too green then to realize you can't expect anything to stay where you leave it, not even an Anne Tyler novel in a room full of rough men.

The din in the common area rose with the body count, rising ceiling high in layers of human noise. It filled the glass-walled space like an ominous, operatic sediment; the overture based on a rumbling *ostinato*, stacked with minor chord threats of "Hey Motherfucker! Don't be touching my shit!"

Little Rosa, the asphalt-voiced cigarette girl, hustled counterpoint through the noise. "Roll-ups two for a quarter!" she shouted. "Marlboro Reds, fifty cents!" Rosa hawked her smokes like a crack-head evangelist, louder by a trick of will or acoustics than the raucous congregation she bull-horned through. The cold-weather crowds were like Black Friday for Rosa's business—her pockets bulged with spare change.

The staff clung bravely to a tenuous illusion of control. Bright young emissaries waded in, armed against indifference with nothing more than clipboards and optimism, their idealism stretched thin as Bible pages.

"Has anybody seen Rodney?" a twenty-something intern asked, scanning the milling bodies. "His case manager's on the way," she said. Overhead, contradiction barked from the loudspeakers: "Attention, gentlemen! Today's case management meetings are canceled due to icy road conditions. I repeat, *canceled*..."

With no pages left to turn, I grubbed through my bag and tried to wish up enough change for a smoke, but no such luck. I slumped over in the folding chair and wondered what to do next—or if anything at all could be worth doing. My senses shut down in the claustrophobic maelstrom, and I nodded out, overwhelmed.

I heard Carter before I saw him, and I only saw him because he stepped on my foot.

His voice broke through the clamor as he shouted into his cell phone, "Yea, we'll talk, man. Between the web pages and the furniture hook-up, we're gonna see some serious bank!" He rummaged through the crowd like a rickety little coat rack, his wiry body overloaded with worn-out gym bags, a pair of sagging backpacks, and tangled, dangling ear-buds. His belongings were the only ballast holding his Mad Hatter energy to the ground.

"Pardon me," and "Sorry, bro," punctuated his conversation as he shouldered through the rabble, his words sporadically choked by a dry, asthmatic hack.

I looked up when he apologized to the old man next to me for stepping on *my* foot. Too tired to be annoyed, I folded up tighter inside my space to make way.

"We need somebody building these websites," he complained. "We should be closing deals already!"

His words fluttered to my feet like loose dollar bills, waiting for me to snatch them up. I could *do* web sites. I'd been damned good at it, back in the day. Showing up sober to client meetings had been problematic, but web design I could handle.

I had to stop him, but it's best to avoid putting your hands on anyone in that room—especially a stranger, and never on purpose—shit will start, for sure. But Carter didn't look like the type to cop an attitude, so before he gathered himself to scurry off, I risked a quick nudge to his elbow.

"You need some web work done?" I asked, clearing my throat. "I heard you saying..."

Sirens and the blasting horn of an ambulance interrupted, knocking the volume of the room from intolerable to excruciating. It was only the second 911 call of the day, and no one paid any mind. The EMTs gathered their equipment and headed for the doors.

Carter drifted for an instant, his attention fixed by the commotion on the street. He looked as if his ride had just arrived. I wondered if he'd heard me.

"Shit. I'm late," he said. "Meeting a money guy for coffee at The Hideout ten minutes ago." With barely a once-over glance my direction, he pocketed his phone and started laying out a business plan. "I need somebody that knows HTML, and somebody to write ad copy for Craig's List. It's a win-win, dollar-wise." He stabbed his palm with an index finger, running item by item through an internal to-do list. "The furniture is drop-shipped—all quality stuff, major manufacturers. We name our price. Undercut everybody and still make a nice percentage on every sale."

A smear on his glasses distracted him, and he wiped them on his sleeve, holding out the bent frames and squinting for missed spots, then stepped back into pitch-man mode: "Do you know there's a five-billion dollar market out there that nobody's touching?"

His nails were dirty, but he was friendly. Civilized.

"I used to design websites," I told him. "And I can do okay with sales copy."

My résumé, served neat, in fifteen words or less.

"I've got a laptop." I offered. "...at a friend's house."

I didn't mention my friend hadn't answered a call in months, but the extra incentive bought some face time. Carter inked his number on his own palm before he realized what he was doing, then shrugged and stuck it out to shake. He smiled around the gnawed pen between his teeth.

"I'm Carter. What's your name?" He hitched up his trousers without waiting for an answer, ready to move on. "We need to talk, but I gotta run."

"Look for you in line tonight?" I ventured.

Carter nodded to confirm the appointment, and trotted toward the exit, load swaying as he pulled a strap higher on his knobby shoulder. He squeezed his bags through the glass doors, bumping past the medics as if they were no more than idlers in his way.

"Make a hole, gentlemen!" a staffer yelled. "*Make a hole!*"

The EMTs hustled upstairs in the elevator and came right back down, their equipment piled on the empty gurney.

A false alarm?

I wasn't sure yet, but it felt like something might actually be *happening*.

If nothing else, Carter had apologized for stepping on me...sort of.

It was forgivable.

The two of us joined forces in the lottery line that evening, shuffling along with a couple hundred guys, all gambling against one another for a spot to sleep indoors. Carter and I both drew good numbers, and the next morning we dug into his plans like pigeons on a pizza crust. We became the Internet marketing wizards of the homeless set, peppering Craig's List with ads for furniture we'd never seen, determined to stockpile our earnings and get the hell out of Dodge. Carter did market research, gathering demographic stats and product info, relishing the crunch of limitless data, while I pounded away at ads, uploading our determination to the 'Net. We'd found a mission, and we had something bigger to do than stand shivering on the sidewalk, waiting for spring.

The winter weather was hard on the homeless that year—like every winter, really, even in mild-mannered Austin. Overnight lows were in the 20s, and the afternoons were just warm enough to trick drunk or unthinking streeters into a frostbitten sense of comfort.

Carter and I spent our days steaming warm in the shelter's second-floor dining room. Our main office was whatever table space we could grab amidst the litter of backpacks, greasy cloth coats, and junk-food wrappers, and we enjoyed a corner-window view of the adjacent parking lot, ringed by anonymous office buildings, St. David's Episcopal Church, and the Austin Omni Hotel.

A quieter crowd peopled the dining room than in the main hall downstairs. Movie lovers huddled elbow-to-elbow around laptop screens, craning to see the latest bootleg download of *Avatar* (dubbed English over Spanish, with Russian subtitles). Gamers hovered fascinated, cheering while a shooter fragged digital enemies in *Resident Evil* or *Assassin's Creed*. Boozy nappers stretched out on the floor around the walls beneath "NO SLEEPING!" signs, their snoring faces buried in backpacks until the staff came in on the half hour to kick their feet and rouse them.

We were too ambitious to waste time on movies or games. We hammered out ad campaigns, frittered over details, and schemed what-if scenarios of easy profit and the fine things we'd own. Some dreams were as simple as a really good bed and a door to lock at night. Other ambitions were more extravagant, like the adolescent fantasy women we swore would share those beds—hot, smart, and adoring, the girls would climb out of our wallets like strippers from a cake. We slurped soup kitchen power lunches of cabbage stew and pimiento cheese on gooey white bread, and packed our bags with stale charity pastries for emergency munchies.

The Omni Hotel teased us from the skyline with its rooftop pool and hot tub. During breaks we'd watch heads bob above the mile-high railing as guests climbed into the bubbling oasis of luxury. The top of the Omni was one of our prime motivators. We swore we'd stay there, play there, and get laid there when the money machine slipped into gear.

Carter was the idea man and corporate cheerleader, but he also had more practical skills, including a gift for scoring free bus passes. He hoarded them for barter, late night ER visits, and desperate escapes. When his cell phone died, he handed me a day pass for a ride-along to the Cricket store.

We boarded the #3 Cap Metro, and while Carter pored over a lapful of notes and crumpled flow charts, I thumbed absently through the previous week's Sunday *Statesman* and dozed away a hangover.

Carter nudged me with a question, and I was surprised when I looked up to find we were rolling through my childhood stomping grounds. Déjà vu stunned me. I'd been a goofy little kid on these streets, and a too-big-for-his-britches teenager. Scenes from lost incarnations unfolded as the stops rolled by, and like "just right" words on the tip of my tongue, I knew they were alive somewhere, but weren't quite real. I'd left myself behind on the way to hometown exile, and somehow, I'd forgotten my own story.

Top Notch drive-in was still flame-kissing burgers on Burnet Road. My family used to eat there on warm nights, cheeseburgers and onion rings filling the back seat of the Delta 88 with gritty salt packets and the aroma of fatty satisfaction. And there was Genie Car Wash, where me and my 6th grade buddy, Peewee, would press our faces against the glass walls to drool over 'Vettes and Beamers gliding sudsy through the machine, following them until they emerged glistening and spotless on the other side.

We passed the decrepit Northcross Mall, most of the shops bankrupt, doors locked. I was more ancient than the washed-out mall, and felt as empty and obsolete. I had run like a wild boy there, in the open fields and hackberry thickets, years before construction began. My bare footprints were somewhere under that parking lot, buried with tangles of kite string and balsa airplanes lost in stands of Johnson grass.

The fogged-over world outside the safety glass grew more and more aloof as the blocks stretched behind us. There were no excited, finger-pointing moments of, "Look, Carter! That's where I hung out when I was just a punk-ass boy!" The #3 lumbered past a world that had given up on my friendship a long time back, and I shrank from it, gutless, like a child too roughly handled to trust any memories of security or safety. These places didn't miss me, or welcome me home. They'd forgotten who I was.

I slouched, hiding a creeping fear of boarding the wrong bus back or getting separated from Carter. I worried we'd be late for dinner at the Salvation Army. If we didn't make it to the shelter by the 6:30 line-up, we'd be locked out for the night. And it was fucking cold.

I didn't have any money, and I didn't have any booze.

I was deathly afraid of my hometown.

As underhanded as any 6th Street hustler, homelessness had become my home, and I was so frightened of the world I'd run out on that I panicked. It was an act of will to stay planted in my seat and white-knuckle it through the trip. I needed desperately to pull the bus over and rush back to the seething concrete womb of the shelter.

Carter was all business across the aisle, making notes of furniture stores we should visit. "Product knowledge, man. Product knowledge," he declared between scribbles. "What's a good word for soft?"

"Sumptuous, plush, luxurious, cushy, comfortable..." I reeled off synonyms and random associations in a preoccupied monotone. "Downy, tender, gentle, giving."

Weak, I thought. *Pointless. Ineffectual. Spineless. Lost...*

"...and don't forget plain old soft," I added.

I was growing numb to Carter's chatter, and I think he knew it.

I needed a drink.

Alcohol never held any appeal for Carter. Outside of hospitals and illness, he'd never done a drug stronger than his inhaler. He understood my alcoholism from a sober distance, letting drop an occasional hint about my stopping into an AA meeting, or suggesting things might go easier if I lightened up on the liquor. He understood though. He knew I'd only fight if pushed.

Like Rosa hawking her roll-ups, vodka spoke louder then than any other voice in the mob, and despite our enthusiasm, the work Carter and I poured ourselves into hadn't produced anything more than Xs on the calendar. Scooping ground-score change from the sidewalk was more profitable. I didn't care much for high profit margins anymore. I just needed four bucks for a bottom shelf pint of Kamchatka.

That afternoon on the #3 marked a tipping point in my mind-set, and my connection to Carter lost out to the urge for accelerated self-destruction. Chasing a buzz took precedence over friendship and sanctuary. I took to sleeping outdoors, or crashing in vacant apartments. There were still times in and out of the shelter, avoiding people I knew, passing through between binges for a shower, a meal, or a mat for the night. My days were too busy for Carter. There was serious drinking to do, and my priorities didn't necessarily involve being human anymore.

I left Carter and our dreams of fat wallets and trophy girls to fend for themselves.

That was over three years ago, and I was still a year away from putting down the bottle. Once the weight of it was gone, I managed to hit escape velocity, up and away from my identity as number 113-119. Like *The Accidental Tourist*, I disappeared myself from that world.

When I was a teenager, living two blocks off the #3 bus route, I had a book entitled *Easy Journey to Other Planets,* by His Divine Grace Abhay Charanaravinda Bhaktivedanta Swami Prabhupada. I never read beyond the back cover, but I'm sure it's as profound as the author's title is long. His Divine Grace's jacket blurb claims that to travel the universe as an enlightened day-tripper is a simple matter of stepping beyond our conditioned beliefs. On the planet where most of us lesser souls live, though, it's no simple trick to shift our weight from one universe to the next, traveling in our own skins, winging it without guidance through this particular life.

There is no *easy* travel between the shifting boundaries of our inner worlds. There are barbed-wire borders to cross, with roadside searches and indefinite detainment, and the inhabitants of neighboring lands often find themselves misunderstood, their once common language faded and forgotten.

Our eyes open from every sleep to an alien landscape, puzzled to find ourselves cast as the outlaw or the community pillar, the lost-cause alcoholic become sober, or waking from the dreams of a younger self in different dress, moving blindly toward the disasters and triumphs ahead. We all live somewhere between what we were and what we're becoming—we should be used to it. But when you awaken to the realization that your image of self no longer applies, when you find yourself standing in the chaos of neither *this,* nor *that*...it's during those nowhere times that the fear sets in.

Our fragile personae exist like colliding galaxies, and when they clash, lives collapse, universes crumble or explode. Sure, you might take the metaphor further and plead that new suns are born from the destruction, that new worlds emerge from the detritus of the old. I believe that's ultimately true, but when you're flying in pieces from the center of the blast, call me then, and tell me how star-like you're feeling at that instant.

Some of the dust clouds of my personal implosions have settled, but not all of them. There will always be unfinished business, a drawer full of unwritten endings and thank you notes. And there's a sky filled with star-bright moments to look back on—I can show you the scars.

Since my years in the shelter, my addictive affections have turned from alcohol to nicotine and caffeine, and I'm secure in a place of my own. The apartment would be beneath most people's standards, but it's above the street, and the funkiness suits me. Today my desk sits by the window, ostensibly so I'll blow the smoke outdoors, but the window seat is most important to sit and stare down from.

Occasionally a homeless person wanders by, carrying their burdens on their back, or pushing an overloaded H.E.B. cart clattering with cans for the recycler. I turn from the monitor while I'm working and watch them pass. The cops don't come through here much, so sometimes the wanderers sit on the curb for a rest, glad to hold still for a minute without any hassle. They go about their business without knowing I see them, and I presume to understand what they're about and what they might be thinking. I feel as if I'm spying from up here, but really, they wouldn't give a damn about one more set of eyes judging them.

I'm like a weekend sailor now, with one foot on the dock and the other on the gunwale, straddling self-definitions as they drift apart. I've weaned myself from soup kitchens and food stamps, but find there's reliable and mysterious safety in a bellyful of cabbage and noodles. And a smear of pimiento cheese on white is a gummy delicacy I never acknowledged in my less grateful years. To this day, I scan the ground for change, and peek over the side of dumpsters as I pass. I get excited when I spot a long cigarette butt on the ground, though I don't usually pick them up anymore. And if anyone spied on me, they'd see a tendency to travel via alleys and across parking lots rather than open sidewalks.

There's still a comfort in the option of hiding, and I always notice the secret places, the holes in the façade where, if needed, a night could be passed unseen.

I remind myself I have plenty to eat, and a door to lock at night.

Some rules still apply, and probably always will: Don't keep your smokes in your shirt pocket. Don't let on you've got *anything,* however trivial or insubstantial, or someone will plot to take it. If you have trouble with the word "No," or aren't willing to lie and say, "Sorry, buddy; not a good day for cash," you'll wind up giving too much away. If anyone asks for a cigarette, tell them, "Fresh out, bro. Maybe next time." The one you're lighting is always your last.

Sometimes when I pass the panhandlers on the street I'll make eye contact and say hello or nod, but most often, I find myself keeping my eyes to the ground.

And I used to wonder how people could so completely ignore another human being.

Carter and I talked a couple of weeks ago, and he sent over email archives of all the ads we'd posted that winter downtown. He saved everything we'd produced.

The furniture project still exists, but on a far back burner. He's got a deal in the works to sell high-end Koozies and water bottles emblazoned with brass, leather, and wood, laser engraved custom logos. Everybody's going to want one. "It's a win-win," he told me. "Huge per-unit profit, and if we move as few as 6 a day, the bank's going to pile up just selling on the street." I could hear the bullet points. "This'll kick ass on the web!"

Carter is still in the shelter, while I'm two years into a new life. He's trying to pull himself up, but I think if he weren't held tight by some internal binding, he would be out here and happy. He lives in a world much larger than mine, as confined by circumstance as he may seem. He's not missing the forest for the trees; he's flying over the canopy, missing both the forest *and* the trees, his eyes on horizons I worry he may overshoot.

Why I worry, I don't know. He'll land on his feet when the time comes. He'll be grinning down from the Omni rooftop, his skinny arms draped around a trophy gal or two, cell phone in one hand, inhaler in the other.

We talked about getting together and I instinctively deflected him from my door.

"Yeah, I'd love to see you," I said. "Let's meet up at the Hideout for a coffee."

We didn't set a date or a time. I didn't even tell him what street I live on.

Boundaries aren't meant to be unbreakable, but I fear mine have grown overly defensive and inflexible. The old life might have claws I can't see, and it may have strength to scratch its way through a crack in the walls of the new. My house is built of Popsicle sticks and Elmer's glue. It could all come apart any second.

I've let myself walk away from more than one good life in the past, stumbling straight off into the worst of shit without even noticing I'd tripped. Am I aware enough now to watch my step? Am I planted firmly enough in this new soil to stand on my own? I think so, but only cautiously. And while caution may keep a lot of valuables locked away in the past, the potential gain may not be worth the risk. I hold my own confidence in suspicion.

Carter must have wondered why I didn't invite him over.

If he did, I hope he knows, as the old saw goes, that it's not him, it's me.

I can't guess what I'd do if I looked out to see Carter marching down the sidewalk, holding last year's Obama phone to his ear and conducting business as usual.

It placates my egoism to imagine inviting him up to hang out and pitch his latest escape strategy. I'd feel beneficent and oh-so-charitable, as if I were holier than my history, but I would worry that Carter might become part of the furniture, or install himself quietly on the shelf like an unread book. It would be a concern that he'd knock unannounced when the days got cold, and if I didn't answer, he'd slip his world under the door into mine.

My selfishness and high-horse arrogance astonish me. If I were to let Carter walk by while I quietly closed the shutters, I might be willing to ride out the guilt for leaving him outdoors, but facing my indifference to a friend burns in my gut like cruelty. I like to think I'm better, at least, than his murderous cousin. I like to believe I'm above rolling away as if he never existed, leaving the battered friendship for dead. But still, I've lied to myself before and swallowed the bullshit whole.

It's my shameful hope that with patient denial, this crisis of conscience will pass and no one will have to notice. Sweeping my callousness back into the past would be an awful relief, like the near miss of an errant asteroid, or hearing news of disaster in a nearby town. But that hope is inescapably and unacceptably selfish. It's the bitter sentiment of "Better him than me."

It's a finer hope that I aspire to—the hope that Carter will fight himself back to the brighter lights of the world, put down his bags, and call me up from *his* new space. He'll either outshine his secrets or come to accept them, and we'll speak the same language again. I think that then I could tell him why I never asked him over, or how I might have even watched without a word as he passed below my window. He might understand well enough then to forgive my failure, and I might understand well enough to forgive myself.

Caitlin Beauchamp

University of Texas at Dallas—Graduate Fiction Award

Solstice

They arrived at the trail head just before sundown, in three old cars carrying more passengers than seatbelts. Moriah emerged thankfully from the stuffy crowded heat of the long ride up through the foothills into the clean cold of a clear evening in late December. It wasn't quite freezing, but her breath shone and her cheeks stung as she put her coat on, looking up at the mountain before them and the small distant sun suspended just above it. It was winter solstice, and she'd come with Forrest and a group of his friends to make their traditional observance, a short steep hike up to the promontory where they would keep watch through the longest night of the year.

Moriah looked around at all the people she didn't know pulling their backpacks and canvas bags and hats and scarves out of the cars, flickering in and out of the circles of blue glare cast by the streetlights through the warmth of the low sun. Forrest knew all of them, but he'd already wandered off. Moriah had grown used to this in the short time they'd been together. Forrest was enthusiastic about anything or anybody new, and he disappeared constantly, reappearing half an hour later without any awareness of the oddity of his behavior.

Moriah walked away from the cars and the laughing, high-spirited people to the edge of the parking lot where the level ground fell away down the side of the mountain. Below her lay the valley, and the lights of her hometown. She knew the shapes of the streets so well she thought she could almost pick out her parents' house, at the edge of a subdivision surrounded on three sides by a few acres of undeveloped fields. In those fields, starred with purple thistles and the deep pink of Echinacea, she'd first begun to learn the names and uses of the plants she found, wandering for hours by herself. When she finished high school she worked and saved for a couple of years so she could move to Johnson City to apprentice under an herbalist. That was where she met Forrest, who was also apprenticing that summer and fall.

She turned away from the valley to look for him, around the small gravel parking lot, the closed up visitor center. The sun had sunk behind the mountain while her back was turned, and the air was suddenly colder. She spotted Forrest at the border of the trees and the parking lot,

109

talking to the only other newcomer in their group besides herself, a girl. She walked toward them. Forrest's back was to her, but she could see the girl's face, looking up into the shadowy woods uneasily. She was very short, with large dark eyes and a row of piercings along the edge of her ear like a small constellation.

"Is it safe up there? In the dark?" the girl asked, looking up at Forrest with her eyebrows raised.

"Here's what you got to remember," Forrest replied. Moriah was close enough to hear him now, though he always spoke quietly. "If you feel afraid of the night, you got to remember it's not out to get you. It doesn't give a fuck about you. Not one cold earthy fuck." The girl laughed and Forrest repeated, "Not one cold earthy fuck." Moriah knew, without seeing, that his face expressed his self-satisfaction for having said something odd or original, a pleasure he was unable to conceal, like a child. She had almost reached them when he put his arms around the girl, backed away from her again, and then kissed her.

Moriah's stomach twisted in shock, and she realized she was standing still, though she didn't remember the moment when she'd stopped walking. She tried to reason her uneasiness away. Forrest was enthusiastic about people, especially people he'd just met. He had a big heart and he forgot what was appropriate. He was probably already a little high. She started walking again, closing the distance between them and put her arm through his. He introduced her to the new girl without any sign of shame in his face, though the girl seemed excited and bashful.

A man in a patched, well-worn coat called everyone to the trailhead. He was the leader, Moriah realized. He looked at the cluster of 20 people gathered around him with friendly confidence.

"All right," he said, holding his hands up, and the people became quiet. "Let's take a moment to center ourselves. What intentions are you manifesting this evening? What energy do you want to carry with you up the mountain?" He paused, then turned and disappeared into the black mouth of the trail, and they followed him. Coming from anyone else, Moriah thought, his speech might have sounded pretentious, but he spoke with an easy sincerity that reminded her of Forrest at his best moments, when they were alone and there was nobody for him to impress—the good evenings, when Moriah brought before him the thoughts and questions she didn't trust anyone else to hear.

Two by two they pushed into the woods, and night fell around them as they walked. The hike wasn't long but in the settling dusk it felt like leaving everything a long way behind, climbing up and into deeper and deeper darkness. Night pressed on them from every side through the dimming trees, the sky watery silver above the black twisted branches. They walked in silence, and a long way off they could hear owls calling as they climbed up the steep slender path. Forrest and Moriah walked together at the back of the line, watching the others ascend ahead of them, scrambling for footing in the dark, moving stiffly through the waist and the arms from the bulk of their coats. Through breaks in the trees, Moriah could see the lights of her hometown in the valley below, which seemed improbably near and bright though she felt so far removed from it.

They had only been hiking for a few minutes when they heard above them a rustling, dragging sound. Moriah heard the click of a flashlight, a thing none of them were supposed to have tonight, and a concentrated circle of yellow light beamed through the thick air of the woods like a cable. It caught on a flash of neon, and then they could see it was a man running down the trail, dressed in a grey and neon yellow running suit and matching shoes. He chugged down the path with pained, huffing determination, the veins along his neck bright blue. The group parted to let him pass and he ran straight through without acknowledging them, as if they were invisible, or as if he were afraid. Moriah looked up the path they were about to climb and saw it as it must have been to him, a living tunnel of growing shadows on a cold night. She turned back and watched him run through the opening of the trail, a square of brightness cut out of the dark trees, leading to a haven of light and space and pavement.

Long before they reached the promontory, the sky and the earth were all the same color, speckled and silvered with snatches of pale light. At first Moriah felt cold to the bone, but the longer she walked up the steep trail the warmer she became. She unwound her scarf and unbuttoned her coat and the rush of cold air on her skin was welcome, and the cold air in her warm lungs felt good and clean. At first they were silent, almost worshipful. But eventually there was a whisper, and then a few more, and then laughter, and then since the silence was broken everyone felt free to talk, even the man who'd made the speech at the trail head. Forrest took Moriah's hand, and their eyes met. Moriah knew what he was thinking, that he was as irritated with the others as she was for breaking the mood of sacredness on their journey. She wondered where the girl he'd kissed had gotten too. She was probably one of the people laughing so loudly up ahead. But she and Forrest would keep silence together, and that solidarity calmed her doubts a little.

After an hour of hiking, they broke free of the trees and spread out on the bare rocky promontory, thatched with patches of stiff dead grass. It was colder now that it was fully dark, now that they were out of the trees' shelter. Someone—it was hard to tell who anyone was—began to gather brush and build their bonfire, though a sign in the parking lot forbade it. It grew from a few flickers in a teepee of grass and twigs into a hot fast fire. They collected sticks and small branches and piles of dried grasses to feed it, and when its first hunger had abated some they gave it a large decaying stump that Forrest found and uprooted.

It was good to be warm again. They settled around the fire and opened their thermoses and boxes and bags of food and drink. Moriah had made lentil stew, rich with curry and coconut milk. Someone passed around anise seed cookies. Everyone had something warm to drink. Moriah could smell yerba matte and dandelion root coffee and chicory coffee and black tea. Moriah and Forrest had black coffee spiked with a generous shot of Bailey's. It was warm going down with the good pure warmth of alcohol on a cold night.

The fire was large and bright enough to read by. Around it people were reading and visiting, and someone had brought a chess board. It was going to be a long night. Already many of them were drunk or stoned. Moriah tried to be patient, and tried not to be possessive, but Forrest kept leaving her alone, and she felt stunned and witless as a woodland creature when drunk people she didn't know tried to talk to her. She looked around for Forrest, and saw him across the fire, on the edge of the circle of the light it cast, talking to the girl from the parking lot again. She watched them for a while. Forrest was doing most of the talking, and the girl was listening to him with rapt attention, standing closer to him than she needed to. Forrest looked happy.

Moriah thought back to when she first met Forrest, on the first day of her apprenticeship in early summer. She'd been reluctant to speak to him at first, partly because she was shy, and partly because she had the habit of silence and passivity that comes to people who spend so much time outdoors and alone. Eventually he introduced himself. He was brown from the sun like she was, with short dark dreads, and he always smelled like the herbalist's stock room, a smell of roots and bitter leaves. She had loved how his face was truly open and empty, like a child's, as if he would take whatever you would give him.

"Come to the woods with me," he'd said. She didn't know him then, and it made her uneasy that she didn't know what all might be implied in the request. She hesitated, looking at his hands and wondering what they would feel like, and if that is what she wanted.

"I'm making you uncomfortable," he said.

"Yes," she answered. For some reason, honesty was easy between them.

In the end she agreed to go. She needed someone to show her the good harvesting spots in the area, and he was willing. He drove her twenty miles outside Johnson City, and whether they were silent or whether they talked she felt at home with him. He pulled off the highway and they drove through a rusted metal gate onto a large overgrown field, backed by wooded hills. He parked beside a collapsed grey barn.

"It's my family's land," Forrest said. "My grandfather was a farmer."

"My grandfather is a preacher," said Moriah. It wasn't especially relevant, but she was in the habit of telling people this. It shielded her. Once people knew that, they made all kinds of assumptions, and some of them were true and some were false, but she didn't care as long as they kept her from having to explain for herself.

They walked across the field toward the woods together. The field had been left alone for two decades now and was full of plants Moriah had never seen anywhere but books. The woods were sparse and full of sunlight and stumps where Forrest's ancestors had felled trees. They walked in silence, the way Moriah liked to walk through woods. Eventually they came on a small pond. The water was clear and brown in the shadow and gold and pearly where the sun fell on it, the thin fingers of light woven through the trees like the warp and woof of course fabric.

"It's the color of your hair," Forrest said, gesturing to the water. "And the color of your eyes." He set down his baskets and tools and sat on the bank and took his shoes off. "I'm getting in," he said. "Come with me."

"But the snakes," Moriah said. "There have to be water moccasins in there."

"Snakes," he said, "don't want us."

"Yes they do," said Moriah. "What do you think they want?"

"They want to be snakes," he said. "You got nothing to do with that. You be a human, they'll be snakes, we'll all marinate in the same goodness."

"Do you know what to do if someone gets bit?"

"I've been swimming here since I was a kid and I've never got bit."

"Do you know what to do?" she asked.

"No."

"Oh."

He stripped off his shirt and his jeans and was about to take off his underwear, but glanced at Moriah, who was studiously looking away, and stopped. His body was skinner than she expected, but more defined, as if someone had drawn the outlines of muscles along his skin with a soft grey pencil. Forrest jumped into the water. Moriah sat down on the bank uneasily. She dug in the mud with her toes. She looked around. The woods were full of good things. Plantain, ginseng, bluet, chickweed. She was hot, and the water looked cool, and after a while it began to seem less and less strange to take off her clothes and get in. Forrest had produced soap from somewhere and was washing himself with his back to her.

"Don't worry," he said. "It's phthalate- free."

She stood up and took off her t shirt and her jeans. She stood on the bank for a while. She could feel streaks of sun on her back like little warm fingers. She wanted him to turn around and see her like that, bare-skinned, with the light in her hair, standing in the woods, but she also didn't, and she jumped in before he turned around. She waded over to him, and he put his hands on her waist.

"Please don't," she said. He took his hand away.

"I think I'm going to love you," he said. "I think I already do."

They had been almost inseparable in the months since then, though few people knew it. Moriah never got around to telling anyone she knew about the relationship. Anyone from her life before she came to Johnson City would be uncomfortable with Forrest, she knew. Through the summer and fall, they'd spent whole days out in the woods and fields. Forrest knew every plant that grew around Johnson city, and he taught her everything she knew about wildcrafting. They would come home sore and tired and aching, their hair stiff with sweat as if it had been coated in rosin. Then Moriah would cook for them, and they would talk about the things Forrest was studying, Native American religious rituals, or Ayurvedic healing, or the folklore of Central America. He was always studying something, usually something Moriah had never thought about before, and she loved to hear him talk.

They had always been alone, the two of them, in the woods, or in their houses. They'd been so secretive, so present with each other, so completely connected in their thoughts and hearts, or that's how it had seemed. But now Moriah watched from the other side of the fire as he kissed the girl again. She turned away from them and walked out beyond the edge of the firelight, to the edge of the rock where she could see the whole valley below. She thought about the man they'd passed on their way up, running down the mountain as fast as he could. He was probably home and asleep in a warm bed. She heard someone walking up behind her and even without looking she knew it was Forrest. He put his hand on her back and they stood silently for a minute.

"Your family lives down there, right?" Forrest asked, pointing to the lights below them on the floor of the valley.

"Why did you kiss her?" Moriah asked, without looking at him.

"Which?" he said.

"What do you mean, which?"

"Moriah, I've kissed a lot of girls. I've slept with a lot of girls. You know that."

"Since you've been with me?"

"I've never been with you," he said.

"Not like sex, like 'being together'," she said, in frustration.

"We're not 'together,' Moriah," he said. She looked at him, trying to find breath to speak in the airlessness that had taken hold of her.

"What are we then?" she asked.

He smiled. "We're just marinating in each other."

"Stop using that stupid word," she said. "You always use that stupid word when you want a quick way out of making sense."

"But that's what we do," he said. "I just want to soak up the good energy we have. Something happens when I'm with you that doesn't happen with other people."

"Apparently plenty of other things happen between you and other people," she said bitterly, and regretted it. That was not how they spoke to each other. "I'm sorry," she muttered. He took her face in his hands and kissed her.

"You love me?" she said.

"Well," he said, hesitating. "Well. I love everybody, really. I guess I should have told you that."

Moriah felt like he'd hit her. She stepped away from him, but he pulled her back.

"Listen to me, let me explain it," he said, talking very slowly, gesturing vaguely with his hands as he tried to think of what to say. His eyes were dark and sleepy and his eyelashes starry in the firelight and she wanted so badly for him to be someone she could love.

"It's like this," he said. He spoke quickly now, the words falling from him. "You know how it is when you see something and you love it and you just get so excited and you just want it. You see a good tree and you have to climb it. Or apples, you can't not bite them. And that look plants have when they are so beautiful and so perfect and the only thing you can do is to dig them up and take them home and you think, thank you, universe, for making this for me. And you know how if you don't take these things there'll be something you didn't allow to become part of you? Don't you sometimes just look out, like when you're at a lake, and you want to drink it and drink it until you're so full you're pissing and drinking at the same time with your throat wide open? Don't you get to the top of a mountain and you just want to stuff the whole fucking universe down your throat, like you want to swallow the sun and get all that light inside you? Don't you know that?"

"Yes," she said.

"Well, that's how I feel about good things, and everything, and you, and other people too. And you're different from other people but then all people are different from other people and I just get so excited about them all and I want everything. I just want to eat everything."

They were both shivering now, away from the fire for so long. He put his arms around her, and she didn't know if it was to warm her, or to warm himself.

"I wish it wasn't like that," he said.

"Me, too," she said. The tears in her eyes made her feel so cold that she made herself stop crying. She wondered how far she would have followed him, if he'd wanted to lead her. She thought she could have tunneled right through the earth if he'd gone in front of her.

"I just love your energy so much," Forrest said. "I just wanted your light inside me. I just wanted my light inside you."

"Are you high?" she asked. He let go of her and stepped back, his hands on her shoulders.

"Your coat," he said, and buttoned it for her.

They were called back over to the fire by the man who had spoken at the trail head. It was time for the ceremony. All of their group gathered around, and someone was handing out small beeswax candles, which they lit from the great fire and held before them.

"Good people, we gather here to bask in the sacredness of the great dark silence," the man said in a raised voice. He was more animated

116

now than he'd been early in the evening, obviously drunk and very earnest. "Quiet your mind," he continued, "observe your heart. Soak up the energy as our world descends into the darkest night. This is a time for reflection and release, so speak your truth, good people. Share with us."

A woman stepped forward out of the circle and began to recite a poem she'd written about the solstice. She had taken off her coat and was wearing only a tank top. The firelight glowed on her arms and chest and the symbols tattooed all over her skin. When she was done there were many more people who wanted to speak. Moriah couldn't pay attention. She looked at Forrest, and at their two candles, bright, brittle points in the dark, one and two out of twenty just like them. How feeble they were, how extinguishable. She looked around the circle at all the strangers, bundled up like refugees against the cold, their faces golden in the firelight and their heads touched with the icy glow of the rising moon. Just beyond them were all the lights of her parents' town.

She remembered how as a child she had watched the moon rise over this mountain from the windows of her parents' house. Their fire was probably visible down in the valley, she realized. She imagined all of the people who loved her walking out into the cold dark streets to wonder at the fire on the mountain, trailing their blankets from their shoulders, a cluster of silent, sleepy witnesses. She had flown so far beyond of the range of what they could imagine. She had stored up so many unorthodoxies in her heart, so many things she would keep to herself so no one would worry about her. What she wanted to tell them all was how, from the ground and from the sky she felt a watchful patience, and the night was all eyes, all consciousness, as if God was keeping vigil with her, in merciful silence.

She could feel Forrest's warm breath through her hat, like fingers winding through her hair. After tonight, whatever had been between them would fade into the darkness of the universe, a thing only a handful of trees and stars and strangers could bear witness to. There would be little evidence. A few books with his initials in them, a dreadlock in the back of her hair that he'd made for her one day on a whim, which she would have to cut out before she moved back home at the end of her apprenticeship. A few plants, a few ideas, the kisses and handprints he'd left on her body that felt so visible, as if they would glow if you just shone the right kind of light on them. Nothing more would remain to testify that she had loved and, in some strange way, been loved in return.

It was past midnight and very cold. When the readings were over and the prayers and chants had been offered, Moriah sat back on the ground before the fire against Forrest's chest and he zipped them both into his oversized hand-me-down coat, his arms in the sleeves and hers tucked inside. They sat and watched the fire fall apart as the night grew colder and everyone began to fall asleep. The logs scattered and shrunk into small charred versions of themselves, flame crowning through the hollows between them.

They sat together deep into the night, never saying a word. The world was so still Moriah thought she could almost see the stars revolving above them, moving patiently through their complex patterns, light into dark, dark into light, one solstice to another. She thought ahead to the morning. Everyone would wake at dawn, and the cold would have worked so deeply into their bones that all the interstitial spaces of their joints would feel frozen. The fire would be a heap of coals, dark but still warm, and a solid plume of hissing smoke would rise when they kicked dirt over it, a hot heart loosely buried in the frosted ground. They'd gather up their thermoses, their backpacks, their blankets and coats and scarves, their cigarette butts and paper sacks. They'd walk back down to their cars silently, beneath the bare trees, and the new sun for which they'd watched the whole night through would barely warm them at all.

Grace Megnet

Lamar University—Graduate Nonfiction Award

The Princess

It was February 19, 1992. I remember the day, because it was my birthday, and I remember the year, because I took my final vows that year in Il Gesu. I spent a year in Rome preparing, together with twenty-seven other nuns of the Missionaries of Charity in Via Casilina.

Men in dark blue suits had arrived a week earlier. We inspected them with forbidden glances as we pushed our wheelbarrows laden with barrels past them, barrels we packed with sawdust so we could light them and heat water for our showers. Our coarse, soot-smudged aprons were a poor match for their expensive, polished shoes. We watched Sr. Agnel negotiate with them. They labored to understand the nun, who, in Indian fashion, moved her head this way and that leaving them to wonder if she meant yes or no. I hoped they knew the word *acha*, which was part of her English vocabulary. But Sr. Agnel did not mind whether they understood her or not. She was meek and humble of heart like her namesake, a true lamb of God. Then Sr. Ludmilla ran down the driveway in her torn plastic slippers and swung open the gate at their command even though nobody had rung the bell.

A constant stream of visitors rang at our gate when Mother Teresa was in Rome: poor people who wanted to see "la Madre," movie stars we could not recognize because we did not read magazines or go to the movies, political dignitaries we did not know because there were no televisions in our convents—we did not even have a radio—religious leaders unknown to us because all the pictures in the *Osservatore Romano* were about the pope. It was read to us on Thursdays. I hated common spiritual reading, especially when Sr. Lorraine read and left out the words she did not know. We were taught to divert our eyes away from visitors should we meet while bringing wood for heating on our wheelbarrows or when we heading to chapel, where we hurriedly adjusted our saris and knelt in neat rows before Mother intoned prayer, "In the name of the Father and of the Son and of the Holy Spirit." But something was different about these tall men in the limo. When they shook Sr. Agnel's hand, she smiled shyly. Then they left our compound and drove the elegant curve down the driveway and out the gate.

"Who were they?" we whispered in that evening as we washed our enamel plates after dinner.

"British Embassy," Sr. Ludmilla shrugged before disappearing into the refectory. We were not allowed to speak after dinner, especially in the washing place.

Our lives continued, and we forgot all about the men, every day listening to Mother's sonorous voice as she started prayer in the chapel at dawn. After prayer we washed our naked feet on the cement slab in the garden behind the kitchen. Freezing in soap scum, we washed our saris, habits, bodices, and headpieces by hand out of a bucket. At breakfast we listened to readings on how to be humble like Mary and holy like Jesus as we chewed on hard bread which we dunked in canola oil and washed down with overly sweet tea. We prayed in the train to Carlo Cattaneo, the night shelter near the Termini, where we made beds while praying flying novenas, Mother's prayer of choice. We folded the stinky pajamas of homeless men, smeared "marmalata" into "paninis," and washed backbreaking, heavy sheets in vats before we hurried back to catch the "trainino" to Casilina 222 where we prayed some more and then ladled a spoon of saucy vegetable stew over our prescribed five spoons of rice, laughing because we were expected to be joyful. When Mother was not visiting cardinals at the Vatican or negotiating with ambassadors for a new foundation—a "house" as we called it – in Ulan Bator or Bujumbura, she gave us instructions on how to be only for Jesus.

"I don't need numbers," she would say, "I need saints. We have now 476 houses in 184 countries, and I need holy sisters. The Holy Father is canonizing a lot of people nowadays, so hurry up and become saints."

"Yes, Mother," we laughed. Then she sent us back to our chores.

We were looking forward to taking our vows and being sent into the world to do something beautiful for God, to assist the poorest of the poor wherever they might be. We dreamt of little children who needed to be washed and taught an alphabet that we ourselves had not yet learned. We would bring the love of Jesus to shut-ins and the love of God to prisoners. We would go to hovels in Africa with beans and rice, feed the starving in Ethiopia, or visit the downtrodden in Paris. We would share our lives with the lepers in Yemen, tell Bible stories to gypsies in Bulgaria, or hold the hands of a young men dying of AIDS in San Francisco. In a few weeks we would be sent into the world with a mission.

We did not celebrate birthdays, but in the chapel during morning meditation I often remembered my mom and the wonderful cakes she baked. I envisioned the shiny eyes of Franny, my younger sister, as we blew out the candles and made secret wishes. That was long ago. I was not supposed to think of home but of my suffering spouse, Jesus crucified, and what he had in store for me once I reached heaven, my true home.

"Tell them, Mother," Sr. Agnel urged during lunch. Mother smiled.

"Tell us, Mother," some of the bolder sisters echoed, as we sat along rough wooden tables.

"Princes Diana is coming to see Mother today," Mother said.

"Princess!" some of us yelled.

"Let us pray." Mother folded her napkin, and we pushed back our benches and made the sign of the cross.

"We thank you, Lord, for these and all the other benefits which of your bounty..."

"I told you – British Embassy," Sr. Ludmilla grinned as we rubbed our enamel plates with a mixture of soap powder and ash.

Nobody slept during the half hour rest which divided our day. We turned and twisted between threadbare sheets; a few sisters even went to the shelf and got their third set out of their bundle, the traditional way of preserving precious clothing in Albania. Mother's ethnic background tended to creep into our otherwise Indian lifestyle. We had two sets of clothes. We wore one while the other hung on the line drying for the next day. The third set was for special occasions only. Some of us wore them only on the day we took our vows, a day which, for my group, was only weeks away.

I stood at the large window on the first floor of the convent at Via Casilina 222, a centuries-old building which the sisters of Divine Mercy had donated to Mother Teresa. The sisters had built a more comfortable place across the street where the Missionaries of Charity lodged the parents of the European sisters when they visited their nun-daughters, which happened rarely. Most of the Indian sisters never had visitors. The rough marble of the window frame reached to my shins. I saw the umbrella pine trees that flanked the driveway from the gate up to the compound. On feast days in August, I liked to crack with a rock the hard husks for the tiny seeds inside the cones and nibble on the tasty nuts while Indian sisters danced to the drumming of our plastic shower buckets. The garden was ripe with anticipation, quiet except for the occasional groan from Giovanni and Giuseppe, two handicapped teenagers in the children's home whom Mother had brought as babies from Sicily. Giovanni was dark, scrawny, and timid, but Giuseppe was feisty and loud. He flailed his arms helplessly when we spooned vegetable mush into his mouth. We often missed, painting his face yellow, orange, or green depending whether the mush was made from potatoes, carrots, or spinach, vegetables that we begged in the general market. Calculating merchants conceded they were *per i poveri*, for the poor.

To the left of the children's home, I spotted a bunch of paparazzi on the roof of the wooden shack where we stored donations for the poor. They had expensive cameras with enormous lenses. Some had rung the bell and wanted to come inside our compound, but Sr. Mary had chased them away. Now they stood atop the flimsy shack with their heavy bags. When the roof collapsed, they fell onto bags of old clothes.

The convent bell structured our day from dawn to dusk in half hour segments, calling us to prayer, work, and meals. Today it rang in happy frenzy as it had only when Mother arrived from India or from one of her many trips abroad.

"She is here. She is here." We straightened our saris and ran over the loose tile in the hallway and down the long, marble staircase, pushing and shoving and giggling.

"Hurry up," Sr. Dorothy said.

"Behave!" Sr. Mary reminded, nervous and red-faced.

We stood in two neat rows of white cotton while the limousine swung into the compound. The front door opened before the shiny vehicle came to a halt, and two polished shoes emerged to open the back door: an elegant foot in an elegant shoe, two model legs, and there she was. We started to sing as we always did when Mother arrived, "We welcome, welcome..." But we were unable to fit five syllables into the "mother" slot but were in perfect unison for "from our hea-ea-eart. We welcome, welcome princess, we welcome, welcome princess, we welcome Princess Diana from our heart."

Sr. Dorothy, behind her dark glasses, frowned when the princess began to shake hands with each sister. We never shook hands. We were not supposed to shake hands. We never held hands. We never touched anyone except for Giuseppe and Giovanni who could not walk, eat by themselves, nor wipe their behinds. Sr. Dorothy told the princess not to shake everyone's hand, but unlike us the princess was not bound by a vow of obedience. She spoke to each of us individually unlike Mother who was always in a hurry and pushed our foreheads, "God bless you,

122

god bless you, godblessyou, bless you, blessyou." The princess's British accent was regal, and we giggled and said "fine," "yes," and "thank you." The Indian sisters moved their heads this way and that. I am sure Princess Diana understood.

Mother waited for her at the door of the house. Sr. Dorothy tried to squeeze into Mother's office, but Mother pushed her out and resolutely closed the door. The princess and the saint were alone. I was surprised that Mother received the princess in her office. Normally Mother received visitors in the parlor or in the garden. Her office was inside the enclosure and, hence, off limits for outsiders. Mother was very strict and would not allow even priests to come inside the enclosure.

"Go to the chapel and pray," we were told, and we settled on the green carpet like a flock of geese. Some of the holier nuns probably thought of Jesus' suffering on the cross as we sat in front of the huge crucifix of Casilina chapel, but I wondered what the princess and Mother were talkings about in that small office with the rickety table and the hard chair. Was Mother sitting on the bed with the white and blue checkered cover as our mistress did when we went to see her to "speak our fault," petty infringements of some rule like speaking and eating out of time or not keeping proper "custody" of our eyes? Was the princess kneeling on the cold floor at her feet as we did? Had Mother taken her chemise from the line on top of the heater, or was it hanging there as it always did? Were they talking about a new foundation for AIDS sufferers? Land mines? The problems of child-rearing in a palace? Mother-in-law issues?

The seconds ticked slowly. Most of us left the chapel and roamed in front of the house where we fingered our rosaries in the hope of another glimpse of our famous visitor. Some sisters leaned over the wall and whispered forbidden conversations. Sr. Mary waddled from the front door to the limousine trying to appease the men in dark blue suits who barked into their two-way radios. One of them even knocked at Mother's office door, reminding her that time was up. Did he not know that Mother took orders only from the pope and God? He was neither despite his polished shoes.

When the door opened, Mother came out and headed straight for the chapel followed by the princess. Mother, bent over in her white shabby sari, her face stern and wrinkled, her step decisive, was nevertheless in charge. The princess whose hairdo was admired by the whole world followed. Did Mother mind that her skirt was awfully short?

"Come out!" Mother ordered the few sisters who remained on the green carpet. They hurriedly crossed themselves with holy water and pressed along the garden wall with the rest of us. Mother bent down to take off her sandals. I had been a nun for nine years, and I knew Mother had no pair. Over the years kind hands had mended them with different colored thread. Now the leather straps lay limply on the mat of the chapel entrance. Next to Mother Teresa's sandals rested Lady Di's designer shoes in black and gold. If I had had a camera, that would have been the money shot.

Mother Teresa and Princess Diana knelt on the green carpet in front of the tabernacle and spent a few moments in silent prayer. When she got back into the limousine, the princess looked sad. The dark blue men barked again into the radio, the gate swung open, and the convent bell rang for tea.

We were excited when with our cups and saucers we huddled around Mother at the refectory table. When she came back from Iraq, Mother had shared the news that Saddam had six look-alikes. "I do not even know if I spoke to the real one," she laughed. She told us about orphans in Bucharest, Enver Hoxha's reign of terror in Albania, and Hillary Clinton's donation of a children's home in Washington, D.C.

"Praised be Jesus Christ," Mother said, the cue that allowed us to speak. Only Sr. Dorothy had the courage to ask about the princess.

"Take another cookie," Mother said and slid the plate with the soggy cookies down the table. This was clearly a special occasion. We sipped our tea and were glad when Mother rose and tea was over. We went about our chores and duties, but nobody mentioned the princess again.

Lucas Jacob, Faith Padgett, and Anna Sudderth

Playing the "Game" and Building Community: Restoring Creativity Structures for Writers Who Are Not in Writing Workshops or Programs

Introduction

Our colleague Adam Cheney of the University of Texas/Dallas has in a presentation discussed the fact that "creative" writing is in fact a process involving a series of reiterative acts, at least two of which function best if one is working as part of a larger community of writers.

Today, our charge is to discuss the ways in which such communities can be created and maintained by writers who are not fortunate enough at a given time to be in formal writing workshops with the deadlines and critiques that come along with such structures—and to acknowledge that sometimes writers do have to work at least briefly in isolation, and to explain how we three create incentives to write at such times.

Finding, Creating, and Maintaining Communities of Writers

We three all acknowledge that we most effectively practice and hone our respective crafts when we are able to be in communities of writers with whom we can share feedback, questions, readings—and deadlines!

And we three are in agreement, probably with most other writers, about the notion that such communities are not necessary just because feedback is helpful or because other writers provide us with new ideas, but also because without them there seem not to be sufficient pressures to make us overcome the daily structures of our lives and just sit down and write. We three all have jobs that far exceed anything like a 40-hour workweek (Lucas is a teacher and administrator; Faith and Anna are full-time students carrying huge workloads), and we all have other commitments that take up huge amounts of time every given week (as arbitrary examples, Faith dances and Anna participates in debate, each of which can easily take a dozen or more hours out of a week that already has little room for anything other than school and, maybe, sleep). Simply put, the path of least resistance is simply not to write.

When formal communities say that we must write, of course, things become much easier.

The three of us first worked together in university-model writing workshops in a K-12 school at which we are privileged enough, in terms of scheduling, credit-hour tabulation, student interest, instructor training, and administrative support, to be able to do such things. An intro-level Trinity Valley School creative writing course meets for over 220 minutes every week and is structured to mandate that students produce work in at least four genres (narrative nonfiction, poetry, playwriting, and fiction) over the course of an academic year; a second-level course has a similar meeting schedule over the course of a single semester, and requires that each student draft and revise at least four major projects, involving at least two of those four genres.

In the intro course, every student's work is formally work-shopped at least once following a protocol like the one found in Appendix A; in the more advanced course, every student's work is work-shopped at least twice, using a more student-driven, and less structured, version of the model. Students are trained, in both courses, in the useful annotating of text with both descriptive and prescriptive comments and questions (see Appendix B). The goal of formal training in annotation and discussion is to keep the focus of a workshop on what is working and is not working toward the apparent goals of a given piece of writing —and why, and how to address the latter—rather than on arbitrary concerns of what a given reader does or does not "like," thereby keeping the writer thinking about process.

In other words, while they are in actual writing electives, TVS writing students cannot help but be working in community with other similarly-interested and similarly-tasked young writers who are specifically charged with providing support and feedback.

But no student can take more than four semesters' worth of creative writing courses at TVS (not counting independent studies that may be done by a very few students during the twelfth grade year; even then, a student will not exceed five semesters' worth of such classes, and only two students have ever been able to schedule that much formal writing study at TVS)—indeed, most interested students can only fit formal writing courses into two or three of their eight high school semesters.

So, how, during the other five or six semesters (and the summers) can students work in the kinds of communities that are so helpful in making one set pen to paper (or fingers to keyboard), especially given that there are time pressures that suggest that writing is going to take away from some other endeavor and/or make one even more tired than one already is? Each of the three of us has a few practices to share from our own experiences.

Lucas Jacob on Modeling Community–Finding and on Being a "Working Writer" in at Least Two Senses of the Phrase

My students know that I spend a lot of time and energy on sending my works out to journals and contests. I show them rejection notices and we celebrate together when I can show them an acceptance letter or a poem of mine in a newly-released journal. I encourage them to do the same on all three counts: to submit their work to audiences both inside and (perhaps more importantly) outside the school; to share their rejection stories; and to celebrate with one another their (frequent) publications and contest successes. It is important for students to realize that they can be, and often already are, part of the larger communities of writers to be found in this city, in the state, in the region, and across the country. I will share with interested students my electronic and physical submission logs, so that those who wish to do so can see models of how to track work that has been sent out "into the world," so to speak.

Similarly, since I find that some of my most valuable experiences as a writer happen in environments like the Napa Valley Writers' Conference (at which I studied poetry with eleven other poets in Camille Dungy's 2013 workshop), I make sure my students know not only about how these things work with "professional" writers but also about all of the similar experiences that are available to them. (Anna will discuss such a case below.) I show young writers at TVS that I am still in touch with writers I know from around the country and the world, not just by keeping my students abreast of my communications and shared projects with such people, but also by bringing writers to campus as short-stay visitors and/or as participants in our annual Young Writers' Conference (to which we invite students in grades 8-12 at five or six area schools).

Faith Padgett on The Game(s)

About 13 months ago, Mr. Jacob and I both realized we were doing less writing than we needed to be, and we were both busy enough to allow our non-writing states to continue indefinitely. To solve the problem, we invented something affectionately called "The Game." Play is simple: one person declares a prompt, something arbitrary like a word or phrase, and those playing must compose a draft based on that prompt. Whoever finishes a draft first "wins" and gets to declare the next prompt. Ideally, players cycle through prompts quickly, hopefully taking a week at the most for one prompt, but this doesn't always happen.

A few months after the creation of the original game, Mr. Jacob and I had left a prompt untouched for two weeks. Mr. Jacob realized that the forces we had established to make us write were no longer working as well, and we both needed to push ourselves further, so he created The Game Part II, or the Lightning Game (see Appendix C for rules). The principle was the same, but the products were more easily churned out at a quickened pace.

Through both these methods, we were able to keep ourselves writing even when school and work would ordinarily rob us of the energy and time to do so. Both versions act as a kind of restorative for mental capacity as well. Because the prompts come out of another person's head, one has to write from a semi-foreign starting point, which allows for unfiltered creation.

The Game as it is known today also involves Part III, in which Mr. Jacob and I must read at least one new poem every night and record it in a GoogleDoc, and Part IV, in which we collaboratively build poems by trading off every sentence.

Part of the fundamental importance of having a game to play is that someone else must play with you. Without the necessary accountability the game imposes, I would write much less, and not feel too bad about it. These little tricks are easily transplanted. I have played the Lightning Game many times with Anna, and with several other writers in the school community, and all have come away feeling more creative and inspired than before.

Anna Sudderth on Writer's Workshops and Conferences

During my sophomore year of high-school, I realized that, as wonderful as the writing community I had built with people like Faith and Mr. Jacob was, I had reached a point where I wanted to increase my exposure to different styles, writers, and methods of teaching. With this in mind, I applied and was accepted to the Iowa Young Writers' Studio, a two week summer workshop for high-school students interested in creative writing.

Attending Iowa brought every fear that I have about my writing to the forefront—namely, that in an unfamiliar community, I might find myself not clever enough, not well-read enough, or simply not talented enough to fit in. Faced with the desire to "prove myself," I at first tried to hide these fears. However, rather than emphasizing perfection, Iowa created an environment where I was forced to let these fears play out. In Iowa, I found a perfect example of why it is so necessary to continue expanding one's writing community: by exposing the vulnerability of my writing process to a group of strangers, I was able to move past many familiar practices I had come to rely on in order to push myself to new levels of creativity.

At the level of actual activities the Studio used as a way to foster creativity, many of the exercises we did were similar to activities like The Game which Faith describes above. The Young Writers' Studio was structured so that, even though the sixty campers were divided into different genre-based workshops, each morning began with the entire camp coming together to participate in a writing exercise called "Stretch." Different each day, Stretch consisted of everything from writing pages of images based on Norwegian punk-rock, to composing bad poetry to elementary school loves, to compiling lists of the top ten things not to do at a best-friend's wedding. There was always an opportunity for people to share their work, unedited, and oftentimes only moments after the writer had put down her pen. This activity highlighted the communal spirit of the Studio, as well as one of the most important realizations I had while there: that one of the best ways to maintain the spark and joy behind writing is to write impulsively, to write in ways that are strange and unexpected, and to share the experience of writing with others.

Making Yourself Write When You Must

While all of the above community-making endeavors can make the writing life feel less lonely and more accessible to any writer (let alone to a young writer falling in love with words for the first time), the fact is that sometimes we are alone with our notebooks, laptops, scraps of paper containing draft ideas, and the like. Every writer is well-served to be meta-cognitive about her own processes—about what helps her to write and about what hinders her. Here, each of us will share a bit of her/his own personal experience in learning how s/he works as a writer.

Lucas Jacob on Self-Created Prompts and Rewards Systems

I try to jot down on scraps of paper or, better, in my phone (or tablet or laptop) any line, image, sound, or idea that might turn into a poem. Pretty much every writer does this. For me, the value of these things comes when I have successfully set aside time to write and I am not with other writers who can push me to an arbitrary target or deadline. If I can pull out a note containing bit of text—even just a few words, a single phrase—I do not feel that psychologically-overwhelming (for me) sense that I am "starting from scratch." I know myself well enough to know that there is a huge difference between my having six or eight words to play with and my having a blank sheet of paper or computer screen in front of me.

I also use my submissions-to-journals work to create incentives. I know that I am far more comfortable sending out work that already exists and has been revised than I am starting a new piece—so I simply do not let myself do much of the former until I can prove to myself that I have done at least a bit of the latter. It's a silly little trick to play on myself...but it often works.

Faith Padgett on Habits and Place-Making

When I first began writing, I struggled with keeping all the bits and pieces together. An image or line would burst into my thoughts, and I would either jot it down someplace I would never find it again, or be too afraid of writing it where anyone else might see it to even pick up a pen. Needless to say, many ideas got lost in my fear of having other people scrutinize my undeveloped thoughts before they were "ready." My advice to anyone confronting the lost-ideas phenomenon is to devote a kind of "sacred space" to the work you are doing. For me, this functions better if it is literal and physicalized (I carry a composition notebook with me everywhere), but it can also function more loosely, as in going to a certain place in the time you have set aside to write, or using a specific font for creative pieces that is distinct from those used for other tasks. By training oneself to recognize specific cues as "now you are going to write" hints, the process of getting started becomes much easier and one feels much less vulnerable.

In talking with other writers about their processes, and in thinking about how I write, I have also seen a fear of being messy, wrong, or inconsistent. The frustration that can stem from believing that a first

130

draft should, in some regard, contain elements of perfection, inhibits creativity. Whether this is feeling the need to put the words down without a single scratch-out/backspace, or assuming that some amount of what is composed should be useable later on, it is a concept that harms our craft. To combat such menacing worries, I further recommend that the "safe space" which one declares separate from judgment by public eyes also be declared separate from one's own judgment at least temporarily. There will be time for revision once one actually has something down.

Allowing ourselves the spaces to write, as well as the time, diminishes our fears about the work so we can just do it. As Mr. Jacob is often reminding me, "Don't think, just write."

Anna Sudderth on Keeping the "Pressure" at Bay

Similar to the "safe space" which Faith describes, my largest goal when sitting down to write is to create an environment where the pressure to produce something "good" doesn't keep me from taking creative risks. To that end, there are two strategies I try to implement when beginning almost every first draft. One of these strategies is that of focusing on elements like sound and imagery, rather than large themes or ideas. This allows me to get at what a poem is trying to say almost indirectly, letting the piece unfold without the pressure of my attempting to fit it to some artificial meaning. The second strategy consists of having several drafts in the works at any given time, so that no single piece becomes my sole focus and receives heightened amounts of scrutiny and criticism.

Another practice I've developed which seems to further both of these strategies is using other people's words or prompts as a starting place for drafts, even if the other person is not someone with whom I am writing or playing a version of "The Game." Not only does this allow me to do away with any preconceived ideas of what a poem should "mean," it also keeps me from hyper-scrutinizing any idea or prompt that I come up with myself. If I try to assign a prompt for myself, I often end up searching for one which I think will produce an effective draft, yet if I promise myself to write about, for example, whatever word my sister happens to suggest, my mind is forced to work creatively within one idea, rather than second guessing itself if the first few lines produced under the prompt don't seem to work.

Conclusion

In the end, what the three of us have discovered in exploring how we manage to make ourselves write when there are so many disincentives for doing so can be boiled down to these three ideas: we do whatever we can to create or to find communities of writers, whether that means traveling to events designated for this purpose or simply formalizing our own extracurricular work with one another; we create for those communities structures that keep the focus on process, not product, even if those structures are playful and simple; and, because we know that sometimes we must work in isolation, we do our best to get to know our own habits so that we can "trick" ourselves into feeling safe to get to work when we hear the voices that tell us that there is no time or that it is too daunting to start a new piece. We hope that some few of our examples will be of use to other writers of all ages and at all stages in their careers, and we hope to hear (and to adopt) techniques from our peers in the Texas Association of Creative Writing Teachers.

Appendix A

Creative Writing, Mr. Jacob
Workshop Discussion Protocol

The writer will remain silent, taking notes, during the conversation.

Workshop members will begin the conversation in an ordered way: going around the circle, first one person will point out a passage in the piece that IS effective (and explain why), then the next student will point out a passage that is NOT yet effective (and explain why) and so on. [Later in the semester, we will be more flexible with this model, but not until everyone has become comfortable as constructive peer evaluators.]

During this structured conversation, any student who wishes to disagree with a point being made or to bring up a different angle on a point being made may do so simply by raising a hand and responding. (Note that "I agree with what has already been said" is not included here. There is no need to repeat what another student has already said.)

Once the structured part of the conversation is over, we will open up the floor to a general conversation that can begin with anyone who wishes to bring up anything at all that will help the writer to revise effectively.

Mr. Jacob will often ask questions during workshop or go to the board to make notes about the conversation. Write these notes down not only for the writer's benefit, but for your own!

Mr. Jacob will, from time to time, go to the board specifically to make note of a "workshop take-away" (which he will designate with a number). These are generalized thoughts about revision that come up through your conversations, and *everyone* is expected to maintain a master list of these throughout the semester for use during the revision process.

At the end of the conversation, the writer will be invited to ask questions of the group (but not to "defend" or "explain" her work: this is not about "right" and "wrong," it's about learning how to think and talk about writing!).

When the process is complete, the workshop will give the writer a round of applause.

Appendix B

Creative Writing, Mr. Jacob
Workshop Annotation Guidelines and Goals

The two terms we'll use all year are "Effective" and "Ineffective."

Nothing is "effective" or "ineffective" unless you can give a reason why.

Always look for both: the effective *and* the ineffective.

No paragraph of prose or stanza of poetry should ever go by without notes on it. There is going to be something effective or ineffective (and in most cases, both) in any given paragraph. Usually there will be several.

There is no "right" number of notes to be made, but consider that even half a dozen notes on a double-spaced page really don't take too much time or space.

At the end of a piece—on the back, or on a separate page, or at the bottom of the last page if there is a lot of space—you must compose an end note at least one paragraph long in which you summarize the 3 or 4 biggest points you feel need to be made about what is effective and ineffective.

Pay attention both to *What is there* and to *What is not there*.

You must sign your name legibly on each piece you read.

Exactly what *the focus will be in terms of "effective" and "ineffective" writing has a lot to do with genre. Always focus on what we've been working on in class. For our first unit, on narrative essays, start here:*

Showing vs. Telling, in general

Use of the Five Senses, specifically, as well as Dialogue, Actions, and Thoughts

The Narrative itself: how does it hold together? does it in fact tell a story? how do the beginning, middle, and end add up?

More specific issues of Structure (including First Line, Title, Ending, and Transitions)

How People and Places are characterized

How Emotions are conveyed

How clearly Memory gets across to Someone who was not there.

Final Note: for you, Grammar matters only if it impacts meaning.

Appendix C

The Game: Part II

I think we can call this "lightning poetry" or "poems arrive really fast" or "now you can't possibly spend too much time thinking, you lunatic" or "writewritewritewritewrite" or something like that.

How it works:

The person whose turn it is to set "the rules" selects from the menu found below. Variable one must be set; at least one, and as many as all five, of the other variables may be added.

Variable One [required]: Time
The timer shall be set for no fewer than 4 and no more than 7 minutes

Variable Two: Content option: "meaning"
What a poem is about or "aboooooouuuut" may be specified

Variable Three: Content option: imagery

An olfactory, tactile, visual, auditory, or gustatory image may be specified

Variable Four: Sound option: rhythm
A specific formal rhythm, or a syllabic pattern, may be specified

Variable Five: Sound option: inter- and intra-word sounds
Rhymes or assonances or alliterations or onomatopoeias, etc., may be specified

Variable Six: Structure option: lines and stanzas
Strictures for line and/or stanza structure may be set

Once the variables have been set (and therefore made into "constants," so to speak), the timer is put in motion and the players of The Game writewritewrite as fast as they can.

Contributors

Pennie Boyett teaches English and journalism at Tarrant County College Southeast Campus where she sponsors the award-winning *Compass* arts magazine. She is a recovering journalist, having worked as reporter, editor, and columnist for the *Fort Worth Star-Telegram, The Dallas Morning News, Grand Prairie News* and *Abilene Reporter-News*. She earned a bachelor of journalism at the University of Texas at Austin, an MA in English at the University of Texas at Arlington and a graduate certificate in narrative journalism from the University of North Texas. She and her husband live in Arlington. They have two daughters and two extraordinary grandchildren.

Jerry Bradley is a member of the Texas Institute of Letters and the author of six books, most recently *Crownfeathers and Effigies* (Lamar University Press). His poetry has appeared in *New England Review, Modern Poetry Studies, Poetry Magazine,* and *Southern Humanities Review*. He is poetry editor of *Concho River Review* and past-president of TACWT. Bradley received the 2000 Joe D. Thomas Scholar-Teacher of the Year by the Texas College English Association and the 2005 Frances Hernandez Award by the Conference of College Teachers of English. He was named Outstanding Alumnus from Midwestern State University's College of Liberal Arts in 2002.

Julie Chappell is professor of medieval and early modern literature as well as creative writing at Tarleton State University. Besides numerous academic books and essays, she has published and read her creative work in various venues. Her creative writing has appeared in several anthologies including *Revival: Spoken Word from Lollapalooza 94; Agave: A Celebration of Tequila in Story, Song, Poetry, Essay, and Graphic Art;* and *Elegant Rage: A Poetic Tribute to Woody Guthrie*. Her first poetry collection, *Faultlines: One Woman's Shifting Boundaries,* was published by Village Books Press in 2013. Her memoir, *The Jail/House Rocked,* is in progress.

Cheryl Clements is a professor at Blinn College and TACWT President for 2014. She has published in *CCTE Studies, Journal of the American Studies Association of Texas, Short Story, Texas Magazine, Southwestern American Literature,* and others. From 2011-2013 she received the prose award from CCTE, and her nonfiction will appear in *Her Texas: An Anthology of Texas Women Writers* (2014). Currently, she is editing two anthologies of nonfiction: *A Shared Truth: What Deepest Remains* (companion to *A Shared Voice*, Lamar University Press) and, with co-editor John Bloom, an anthology of essays about Texas Monthly. Cheryl lives in College Station with her husband, John Schaffer, and daughter, Marlene.

Jerry Craven's most recent novel and his 26th published book is *The Wild Part*. A sequel, *Women of Thunder,* is upcoming from TCU Press. He has taught for seven universities in three countries. Currently, he serves as press director for Lamar University Press and Ink Brush Press, and he is editor-in-chief for the literary quarterly *Amarillo Bay*. He lives with his wife, Sherry, in Jasper, Texas. www.jerrycraven.com

Terry Dalrymple teaches literature and creative writing at Angelo State University in San Angelo. A member of TACWT since the mid-80s, he is also a member of the Texas Institute of Letters. He has published several books and has most recently been included in *Texas 5 X 5*, a collection of five stories each by five Texas writers released by Stephen F. Austin University Press.

Thomas de la Cruz was born in the small town of Blythe, California. When he was four, his family moved to yet another small town—Elsa, Texas. He is very proud de ser hijo del pueblo and writes his stories so that his brothers and sisters can read them. In 2008 he received his B.A from the University of Texas – Pan American, and in 2013 he received his Masters of Fine Arts in Creative writing from the same university. His writing has appeared in the journal *Gallery* and in the book *¡Arriba Baseball!* published by VAO Publishing in 2013.

Sybil Pittman Estess lives in Houston, where for 35 years she has written and taught. She is the author, co-author, or editor of six books, including four books of her own poetry. She has published in many journals, including *The Paris Review, The Texas Review, Borderlands, The Langdon Review of the Arts in Texas*, and other national journals. She is at work on a book of New and Selected Poems, and also a memoir of growing up in Mississippi in the 1940s and 50s. Sybil has a Ph.D. from Syracuse University and was one of eight finalists for Poet Laureate of Texas in 2009.

Lucas Jacob's work has appeared or is forthcoming in dozens of literary journals, including *Southwest Review, Barrow Street, Evansville Review,* and *Chautauqua.* A past winner of the Gival Press Tri-Language Poetry Prize, he was a finalist for the 2012 Fish Poetry Prize, a semi-finalist for the 2012 Norman Mailer Award in short fiction, and a finalist for the 2013 Arts & Letters Poetry Prize. He serves as Dean of Learning and Curriculum, Chair of the Department of English, and instructor in English and Creative Writing at the Trinity Valley School in Fort Worth, Texas.

Janet McCann has published her poems in such journals as *Kansas Quarterly, Parnassus, Nimrod, Sou'wester, New York Quarterly, Tendril, Poetry Australia.* She has won five chapbook contests, sponsored by Pudding Publications, Chimera Connections, Franciscan University Press, Plan B Press, and Sacramento Poetry Center. A 1989 NEA Creative Writing Fellowship winner, this crone poet has taught at Texas A & M University since 1969. Her most recent poetry collection is *The Crone at the Casino* (Lamar University Press, 2013).

Nathanael O'Reilly was born and raised in Australia. He now resides in Texas and teaches at TCU in Fort Worth. He is the author of two chapbooks, *Suburban Exile: American Poems* (2011) and *Symptoms of Homesickness* (2010), both published in Australia by Picaro Press. Over one hundred of his poems have been published in journals and anthologies around the world, including *Antipodes, Australian Love Poems 2013, Cordite, LiNQ, Blackmail Press, Harvest, Transnational Literature, Mascara, Windmills, Postcolonial Text, Red River Review, Tincture,* and *Social Alternatives.*

Faith Padgett is a senior at Trinity Valley School, where she is Co-President of the literary magazine. Her poems have appeared in the Poetry Society of Texas' 2012 student anthology and are forthcoming in *Hanging Loose.* Her work has received honorable mention in the Nancy Thorp Poetry Contest, first place and honorable mention in the TVS John Graves Award, and several recognitions from the Scholastic Writing Awards. When not scribbling poems in her notebook, she dances, teaches ballet to four-year-olds, and conducts meetings of the school's diversity club. She was recently named a YoungArts finalist and will attend YoungArts week.

Dave Parsons, 2011 Texas Poet Laureate, is recipient of an N.E.H. Dante Fellowship to the SUNY, the French/American Legation Poetry Prize, Texas Review Poetry Prize, and Baskerville Publisher's Prize. He was inducted into The Texas Institute of Letters in 2009. After serving in the U.S.M.C. Reserve as a Squad Leader in a rifle Company and a Recon-Scout Boat Team Leader, he attended The University of Texas and Texas State University. After 15 years in advertising and coaching at Bellaire High School, he received his M.A. from the University of Houston. He has published four collections and teaches at LSC–Montgomery.   www.daveparsonspoetry.com

Matthew Pitt lives in Fort Worth, where he is Assistant Professor of English at TCU. His first short story collection, *Attention Please Now*, won the Autumn House Fiction Prize. It was later a winner of Late Night Library's Debut-litzer Prize and finalist for the Texas Writers League Book Award. Matthew's short fiction has received numerous honors and awards, and has appeared in over thirty journals, magazines, and anthologies, including *Oxford American*, *BOMB*, *The Southern Review, Conjunctions, Epoch, Cincinnati Review*, and *BEST NEW AMERICAN VOICES*.

Moumin Quazi teaches creative writing at Tarleton State University where he also serves as the Director of Graduate Studies in English. He serves on the Advisory Board of the *South Asian Review*, edits *CCTE Studies* and the book series, "South Asian Art, Literature, and Culture Studies" (Peter Lang Publishing), co-edits *Langdon Review of the Arts in Texas*, and co-organizes the Langdon Review Weekend. In 2012, his poem "Migrant Birds" was published in a Prentice Hall literature textbook. In 2013, he moderated the judging for the Alfredo Del Moral Foundation Award (created by Sandra Cisneros, in honor of her father). He is presently finishing his first book, a collection of poetry, fiction, and memoir.

Charlotte Renk's poems and short stories arise from reflections on long walks in woods behind her cabin. She taught English, Creative Writing, and Humanities in Athens, Texas for thirty years. She has published in such journals as *Kalliope, Mochila Review, New Texas, Concho River Review, Sow's Ear, Langdon Review of the Arts in Texas, and Southwest Review*. Eakin Press published her prizewinning collection, *These Holy Hungers: Secret Yearnings from an Empty Cup*

(2009), and Poetry in the Arts published her book, *Solidago, An Altar to Weeds* (2010). Five new poems will appear in *Her Texas* this year.

Marilyn Robitaille, Associate Professor in the Department of English and Director of International Programs at Tarleton State University in Stephenville,Texas, co-edits *The Langdon Review of the Arts in Texas* and co-organizes the annual *Langdon Review* Weekend in Granbury, Texas. Her work has been published in *New Texas, English Journal, CCTE Studies,*and most recently, in the forthcoming *Her Texas: An Anthology of Texas Women Writers*. Her film reviews are featured weekly in the *Stephenville Empire Tribune*. She is Past-president of Study Texas, a consortium committed to promoting Texas as a destination for international students. She also serves on the editorial staff of the *Journal of International Students*.

Jim Sanderson has published two collections of short stories, an essay collection, and seven novels. Most recently, *Trashy Behavior*, a short story collection, will appear in 2013, and *Nothing Lose* and *Hill Country Property* will appear in 2014. He has published over eighty short stories, essays, and scholarly articles. Most recently, his short story, "Bankers" won the 2012 Texas Institute of Letters' Kay Cattarulla Award for best story by a Texan or about Texas. Jim is currently serving as Chair of the Department of English and Modern Languages at Lamar University.

Anna Sudderth is currently a junior at Trinity Valley School. She received several Gold Key Awards in the 2012 and 2013 Scholastic Art and Writing Awards for her work in poetry and short fiction. Her work has also placed in numerous competitions for the Poetry Society of Texas, and one of those poems was selected for national consideration in the Manningham Competition. She also received Honorable Mention for her submission to Hollins University's Nancy Thorpe competition. Over the past summer, she attended the Iowa Young Writer's Conference at the University of Iowa.

Sidney Thompson is the author of the short story collection *Sideshow*. His fiction, twice nominated for the Pushcart Prize, has appeared in *The Southern Review, Carolina Quarterly, Prick of the Spindle, Grey Sparrow Journal, Clapboard House, Ragazine.CC, Danse Macabre, Ostrich Review, TINGE Magazine, 2 Bridges Review,*

Flash: The International Short-Short Story Magazine, NANO Fiction, Atticus Review, the NewerYork's Electric Encyclopedia of Experimental Literature, The Story Shack, Connu ("The Liars Notebook"), *Beetroot Journal* ("Chemical"), and elsewhere. He lives in Denton, Texas, where he teaches creative writing at Texas Woman's University.

Terri M. Tucker's poetry and prose have appeared in various literary journals and publications, including the *San Antonio Express-News, S.A. Scene Monthly, Concho River Review, New Texas, and descant. In 2013, she* presented creative nonfiction and poetry at East Central University of Oklahoma's Scissortail Literary Festival and at TYCA Southwest and TACWT conferences. Currently, she is working on a collection of short stories that reflect characters from rural parts of Texas. Tucker is a professor of English and the Chair of the Humanities and Fine Arts Division at Southwest Texas Junior College in Uvalde, Texas.

Dan Williams is a closet poet. He is also the Director of TCU Press and the Honors Professor of Humanities in the John V. Roach Honors College at TCU. A specialist in early American print culture, he recently published a novel, *The Lords of Leftovers* (Ink Brush Press, 2013).

Texas Literary Journals

This list is maintained and updated on our website:
www.writingtexas.org

Amarillo Bay
URL: http://www.amarillobay.org
Publisher: Robert Whitsitt, Independent, online
Year Founded: 1999
Description/Editorial Focus: *Amarillo Bay* intends to be the online literary magazine containing the finest modern literature. We seek the highest quality fiction, poetry, and creative nonfiction written in English anywhere in the world. Our editors will consider submissions from both unpublished and established authors. We have published 4 issues per year since 1999; as a new issue comes out, the previous one joins what is now a huge on-line anthology of past issues. Currently we have "subscribers" in 27 states and 10 countries.
Publications Per Year: 4
Submission Policy:
Accepts Electronic Submissions: Yes
Accepts Simultaneous Submissions: Yes
Accepts Unsolicited Submissions: Yes
Contact Information:
Submission guidelines: http://www.amarillobay.org/submit/submit.htm
Robert Whitsitt, publisher and technical editor

American Letters & Commentary
URL: amletters.org
Publisher: Department of English at The University of Texas, San Antonio
Year Founded: 1988
Description/Editorial Focus: *American Letters & Commentary* is an eclectic literary magazine featuring innovative and challenging writing in all forms. Each annual issue features a substantial and diverse selection of fiction, poetry, essays, translation, and critical opinion by renowned and up-and-coming writers.
Publications Per Year: Annual
Submission Policy:
Accepts Electronic Submissions: No
Accepts Simultaneous Submissions: Yes
Accepts Unsolicited Submissions: Yes
Contact Information:
David Vance, Co-editor
P.O. Box 830365
San Antonio, TX 78283
amerletters@satx.rr.com

American Literary Review
URL: english.unt.edu/alr/
Publisher: Department of English at the University of North Texas, Denton
Year Founded: 1990

Description/Editorial Focus: Publishes poetry, fiction, and nonfiction by writers at all stages in their careers.
Publications Per Year: Biannual
Submission Policy:
Accepts Electronic Submissions: Only through online Submission Manager
Accepts Simultaneous Submissions: Yes
Accepts Unsolicited Submissions: Yes
Contact Information:
PO Box 311307
University of North Texas
Denton, TX 76203-1307
Miroslav Penkov and Barbara Rodman, fiction editors
Bonnie Friedman, nonfiction editor
Bruce Bond and Corey Marks, poetry editors
americanliteraryreview@gmail.com

American Short Fiction
URL: www.americanshortfiction.org/
Publisher: American Short Fiction, Inc., Austin
Year Founded: 1991
Description/Editorial Focus: Nationally-circulated literary magazine. Publishes short fiction, novel excerpts, and novellas. *ASF* Strives to discover and publish new fiction in which transformations of language, narrative, and character occur swiftly, deftly, and unexpectedly. We are drawn to evocative language, unique subject matter, and an overall sense of immediacy. In addition to its print magazine, American Short Fiction also publishes stories (under 2000 words) online.
Publications Per Year: Triannual
Submission Policy:
Accepts Electronic Submissions: Yes
Accepts Simultaneous Submissions: Yes
Accepts Unsolicited Submissions: Yes
Contact Information:
Rebecca Markovits & Adeena Reitberger, Editors
P.O. Box 4152
Austin, TX 78751
editors@americanshortfiction.org

Analecta
URL: analectajournal.tumblr.com
Publisher: Senate of College Councils at University of Texas at Austin
Year Founded: 1974
Description/Editorial Focus: *Analecta* is the official Literary and Arts Journal at the University of Texas. An entirely student-run publication, Analecta is produced by a small group of undergraduate students committed to finding exceptional work by both undergraduate and graduate students at UT. Analecta features a manifold collection of poetry, prose (both essays and fiction), dramatic works, and visual arts.

Analecta's mission is to produce a journal of art and literature that poignantly reflects the diversity of experience and overwhelming talent present in the UT community. Analecta is an agency of the UT Senate of College Councils.
Publications Per Year: Annually
Accepts Electronic Submissions: Yes
Accepts Simultaneous Submissions: N/A
Accepts Unsolicited Submissions: Yes
Contact Information:
analecta.ut@gmail.com

Aries: Journal of Art and Literature
URL: twuaries.wordpress.com
Publisher: Department of Languages and Literature at Texas Wesleyan University, Fort Worth
Year Founded: 1986
Description/Editorial Focus: *Aries* is an international literary magazine. Original, unpublished poetry (including poetry written in Spanish and translated), short fiction, one-act plays, black and white photography, and art are showcased in the journal.
Publications Per Year: Annual
Submission Policy:
Accepts Electronic Submissions: No
Accepts Simultaneous Submissions: Yes
Accepts Unsolicited Submissions: Yes Contact Information:
Aries
c/o Dr. Stacia Neeley, General Editor
Texas Wesleyan University
Department of Languages and Literature
1201 Wesleyan
Fort Worth, TX 76105-1536
Dr. Stacia Neeley
sneeley@txwes.edu

Bat City Review
URL: batcityreview.com/
Publisher: Center for Writers, Department of English University of Texas, Austin
Year Founded: 2004
Description/Editorial Focus: Publishes fiction, poetry, and non-fiction.
Publications Per Year: Annual
Submission Policy:
Accepts Electronic Submissions: Through online Submission Manager
Accepts Simultaneous Submissions: Yes
Accepts Unsolicited Submissions: Yes
Contact Information:
Bat City Review
Department of English
The University of Texas at Austin
1 University Station B5000
Austin, TX 78712

Jeff Bruemmer, editor
fiction@batcityreview.com

Bayousphere
URL: http://prtl.uhcl.edu/portal/page/portal/BAY/Bayousphere
Publisher: The University of Houston – Clear Lake
Year Founded: 2002?
Description/Editorial Focus: The University of Houston-Clear Lake publishes *Bayousphere* to provide a creative outlet for its students and the community. Students enrolled in Magazine Publication produce the literary art magazine as part of the course curriculum.
Publications Per Year: Annual
Submission Policy:
Accepts Electronic Submissions: No
Accepts Simultaneous Submissions: Yes
Accepts Unsolicited Submissions: Yes
Contact Information:
Bayousphere
c/o Dr. Hunter Stephenson
University of Houston-Clear Lake
2700 Bay Area Blvd., Box 339
Houston, TX 77058

Borderlands: Texas Poetry Review
URL: www.borderlands.org/
Publisher: supported in part by The City of Austin through the Economic Growth & Redevelopment Services Office/Cultural Arts Division
Year Founded: 1992
Description/Editorial Focus: Publishes poetry as well as reviews, essays and visual art series. We publish work of merit that exhibits social, political, geographical, historical or spiritual awareness. We are open to traditional and experimental forms.
Publications Per Year: Biannual
Submission Policy:
Accepts Electronic Submissions: No
Accepts Simultaneous Submissions: No
Accepts Unsolicited Submissions: Yes
Contact Information:
Ramona Cearley, Director
PO Box 33096
Austin, TX 78764
borderlandspoetry@hotmail.com

Callaloo
URL: callaloo.tamu.edu
Publisher:
Year Founded: 1976
Description/Editorial Focus: *Callaloo*, the premier journal of arts, letters, and cultures of the African Diaspora, publishes original works by, and studies of, black writers

145

worldwide. Recently ranked 13th in Every Writer's Resource's Top 50 Literary Magazines, the journal offers an engaging mixture of fiction, poetry, critical essays, interviews, drama, critical studies, and visual art. Frequent annotated bibliographies, special issues dedicated to major writers and prominent social and cultural themes, and full-color, original artwork and photography are some of the features of this highly acclaimed international showcase of arts and letters. Annual subscriptions will now include a fifth issue titled Callaloo Art.

Publications Per Year: 5 times
Submission Policy:
Accepts Electronic Submissions: Through Submission Manager
Accepts Simultaneous Submissions: No
Accepts Unsolicited Submissions: Yes
Contact Information:
Callaloo
4212 TAMU
Texas A&M University
College Station, TX 77843-4212
Phone: (979) 458-3108
Fax: (979) 458-3275
callaloo@tamu.edu

Camera Obscura
URL: www.obscurajournal.com
Publisher: Sfumato Press, Addison
Year Founded: 2009
Description/Editorial Focus: Showcasing the work of both established and emerging artists, Camera Obscura Journal is a full-color volume of contemporary literature and photography, intended to be read and enjoyed, as well as displayed. The writing and photography is selected on the individual merit of each piece, creating an organic collaboration of art forms.
Publications Per Year: Semiannual
Submission Policy:
Accepts Electronic Submissions: Yes
Accepts Simultaneous Submissions: Yes
Accepts Unsolicited Submissions: Yes
Contact Information:
Camera Obscura
c/o Sfumato Press
PO Box 2356
Addison, TX 75001
M. E. Parker, editor in chief
editor@obscurajournal.com
obscurajournal.com
semiannual

Carcinogenic Poetry
URL: www.carcinogenicpoetry.com
Publisher: Virgogray Press, Austin

Year Founded: 2009
Description/Editorial Focus: *Carcinogenic Poetry* has proven to be a base for the underground and independent poets and writers who want to read poetry and get their poetry read. Since its inception in the winter of 2009, *Carcinogenic Poetry* has featured over 100 poets and has been visited around the world by 1000s of readers and literary enthusiasts! *Carcinogenic Poetry* even boasts an annual print anthology! The motto at *Carcinogenic Poetry* is, "The truth is to lies like cancer!"
Publications Per Year: N/A
Submission Policy:
Accepts Electronic Submissions: Yes
Accepts Simultaneous Submissions: Yes
Accepts Unsolicited Submissions: Yes
Contact Information:
Michael Aaron Casares, publisher/editor
Austin, TX 78744
michael.aaron.casares@gmail.com

Carve Magazine
URL: carvezine.com
Publisher: Independent, Dallas
Year Founded: 2002
Description/Editorial Focus: *Carve* seeks to publish outstanding literary fiction and to promote the writers we publish, helping both new, emerging, and established authors reach a wider literary audience. This is achieved through sharing their stories across a variety of publication mediums: online, print, e-readers, and more.
Publications Per Year: Quarterly
Submission Policy:
Accepts Electronic Submissions: Yes
Accepts Simultaneous Submissions: Yes
Accepts Unsolicited Submissions: Yes
Contact Information:
Carve Magazine
PO Box 701510
Dallas, TX 75370
Matthew Limpede, editor
managingeditor@carvezine.com
editor@carvezine.com

CCTE Studies
URL: N/A; see CCTE website: cctetexas.org/
Publisher: Conference of College Teachers of English (CCTE)
Year Founded: N/A
Description/Editorial Focus: peer-reviewed scholarly journal. Publishes the best conference papers by CCTE members plus the prize-winning TCEA paper. Your subscription is part of your membership. CCTE welcomes scholarly papers, creative writing, and panels in literature and language, including linguistics, film, popular culture, rhetoric, composition, ESL, and teaching these areas. CCTE works closely with the Texas College English Association (TCEA), an affiliate of the national College English

Association. TCEA provides several sessions for the annual spring conference of CCTE, and the prize-winning TCEA paper is honored with publication in CCTE Studies. TCEA also presents the Joe D. Thomas CEA Outstanding Service Award to an outstanding colleague each year.

Publications Per Year: Annual
Submission Policy:
Accepts Electronic Submissions: Only
Accepts Simultaneous Submissions: No
Accepts Unsolicited Submissions: Yes
Contact Information:
ccte@suanna.org

Concho River Review
URL: www.angelo.edu/dept/english_modern_languages/concho_river_review.php
Publisher: Department of English and Modern Languages at Angelo State University, San Angelo
Year Founded: 1987
Description/Editorial Focus: *CRR* has prided itself on publishing some of the Southwest's finest short fiction, non-fiction and poetry, submitted by both emerging and established authors. While CRR always will maintain its connection to the Southwest region and its rich culture, it now is accepting literature of the broader South.
Publications Per Year: Biannual
Submission Policy:
Accepts Electronic Submissions: Yes
Accepts Simultaneous Submissions: Yes
Accepts Unsolicited Submissions: Yes
Contact Information:
Dr. Erin Ashworth-King, editor
Concho River Review
Angelo State University
ASU Station #10894
San Angelo, TX 76909-0894
325-486-6139
crr@angelo.edu

Dappled Things
URL: dappledthings.org
Publisher: Bernardo Aparicio, Arlington
Year Founded: 2006
Description/Editorial Focus: *Dappled Things* is a literary magazine dedicated to providing a space for emerging writers to engage the literary world from a Catholic perspective. The magazine is committed to quality writing that takes advantage of the religious, theological, philosophical, artistic, cultural, and literary heritage of the Catholic Church in order to inform and enrich contemporary literary culture. *DT* is a journal of ideas, art, and faith, publishing fiction, poetry, interviews, essays, visual art, and more.
Publications Per Year: Quarterly
Submission Policy:
Accepts Electronic Submissions: Yes, only through Submittable

Accepts Simultaneous Submissions: Yes
Accepts Unsolicited Submissions: Yes
Contact Information:
Bernardo Aparicio, publisher
600 Giltin Drive
Arlington, TX 76006
dappledthings.aparicio@gmail.com
dappledthings.editor@gmail.com

descant
URL: descant.tcu.edu
Publisher: TCU Department of English, Fort Worth
Year Founded: N/A
Description/Editorial Focus: A forum for fiction and poetry, descant seeks high-quality work in either innovative or traditional forms. descant specifies no particular subject matter or style.
Publications Per Year: Annual
Submission Policy:
Accepts Electronic Submissions: N/A
Accepts Simultaneous Submissions: No
Accepts Unsolicited Submissions: Yes
Manuscripts considered from September 1 through April 1
Contact Information:
descant
c/o TCU Department of English
Box 297270
2850 S. University Dr.
Fort Worth, TX 76129

The Dirty Goat
URL: www.thedirtygoat.com/index.html
Publisher: Host Publications, Austin
Year Founded: 1988
Description/Editorial Focus: Bilingual magazine featuring material from countless areas around the globe. Each issue contains poetry, prose, drama, interviews and visual art in an 8" X 10" format.
Publications Per Year: Annual
Submission Policy:
Accepts Electronic Submissions: No
Accepts Simultaneous Submissions: No
Accepts Unsolicited Submissions: No
Contact Information:
Host Publications (Austin)
1000 East 7th Street, Suite 201
Austin, TX 78702
Tel: 512-236-1290
Fax: 512-236-1208
Susan Lesak, director of fulfillment:

slesak@hostpublications.com
Joe W. Bratcher III, president:
jbratcher@hostpublications.com

The First Line
URL: www.thefirstline.com
Publisher: Blue Cubicle Press, LLC, Plano
Year Founded: 1999
Description/Editorial Focus: The purpose of *The First Line* is to jump start the imagination – to help writers break through the block that is the blank page. Each issue contains short stories that stem from a common first line; it also provides a forum for discussing favorite first lines in literature. *The First Line* is an exercise in creativity for writers and a chance for readers to see how many different directions we can take when we start from the same place. We are open to all genres. We try to make *TFL* as eclectic as possible.
Publications Per Year: Quarterly
Submission Policy:
Accepts Electronic Submissions: Yes
Accepts Simultaneous Submissions: No
Accepts Unsolicited Submissions: Yes
Contact Information:
The First Line
PO Box 250382
Plano, TX 75025-0382
David LaBounty, editor
david@thefirstline.com

Foxing Quarterly
URL: www.foxingquarterly.com
Publisher: Independent, Austin
Year Founded: 2012
Description/Editorial Focus: *Foxing Quarterly: A Print-Only Creative Space for Writers and Artists.* Our goal is to deliver inventive, well-cultivated nourishment to the lit, art, and print community. Our journal publishes, but is never limited to: Short Fiction, Poetry, Comics, Nonfiction, and Visual Art. The magazine has an online supplement: *Fox Hunting*. It is our mission to promote and support the greater literary community. Here, we'll continue to bring focus to emerging writers and cartoonists, micro-publishers, independent bookstores, and much more.
Publications Per Year: Quarterly
Submission Policy:
Accepts Electronic Submissions: Yes
Accepts Simultaneous Submissions: Yes
Accepts Unsolicited Submissions: Yes
Contact Information:
Daniel Mejia, editor
editor@foxingquarterly.com

Front Porch Journal
URL: www.frontporchjournal.com
Publisher: MFA program, Department of English at Texas State University, San Marcos, online
Year Founded: 2006
Description/Editorial Focus: Publishes poetry, fiction, nonfiction, reviews, and interviews. They also feature a video and audio archive, which showcases celebrated authors reading and discussing their work.
Submission Policy:
Accepts Electronic Submissions: Only through the online Submission Manager
Accepts Simultaneous Submissions: Yes
Accepts Unsolicited Submissions: Yes
Contact Information:
Front Porch
MFA Program
Department of English
Texas State University
601 University Drive
San Marcos, TX 78666
frontporchjournal@gmail.com

Glass Mountain
URL: www.glassmountainmag.com
Publisher: Department of English at University of Houston, Houston
Year Founded: 2006
Description/Editorial Focus: *Glass Mountain* was founded when several undergraduate students at the University of Houston combined their creativity and skills to start a journal that would be the counterpart of Gulf Coast, the journal edited by graduate creative writing students at UH. We're a national journal that accepts poetry, prose, and art!
Publications Per Year: N/A
Submission Policy:
Accepts Electronic Submissions: Yes
Accepts Simultaneous Submissions: Yes
Accepts Unsolicited Submissions: Yes
Contact Information:
Glass Mountain
University of Houston
Department of English
Houston, TX 77204
glassmountaineditors@gmail.com

Gulf Coast
URL: gulfcoastmag.org/
Publisher: Department of English at University of Houston, Houston
Year Founded: 1986
Description/Editorial Focus: Student-run, nationally-distributed journal housed within the University of Houston's English Department. The print journal comes out each April and

October and also encourages fine art submissions as well as fiction, essays, poetry, interviews and reviews.
Publications Per Year: Semiannually
Submission Policy:
Accepts Electronic Submissions: Yes
Accepts Simultaneous Submissions: Yes
Accepts Unsolicited Submissions: Yes
Contact Information:
Gulf Coast
Department of English
University of Houston
Houston, TX 77204-3013
Nick Flynn, faculty editor
editors@gulfcoastmag.org

Hothouse Literary Journal
URL: uthothouse.tumblr.com
Publisher: Undergraduate English Department of the University of Texas at Austin.
Year Founded: 2011?
Description/Editorial Focus: *Hothouse Literary Journal* features prose, poetry, and nonfiction. The magazine is run by and features the work of University of Texas undergraduate English majors. The online version for 2012–2013 is now available on issuu.com (http://bit.ly/14MzJnv).
Publications Per Year: Annual
Submission Policy:
Accepts Electronic Submissions: Yes
Accepts Simultaneous Submissions: Yes
Accepts Unsolicited Submissions: Only English majors may submit.
Contact Information:
Hothouse EIC Melissa Ragsdale
uthothouse.submissions@gmail.com
uthothouse.editor@gmail.com

Huizache
URL: www.centrovictoria.net/huizache.html
Publisher: CentroVictoria: Center for Mexican American Literature and Culture
Year Founded: 2011
Description/Editorial Focus: CentroVictoria is excited to announce its new literary magazine, *Huizache*, featuring poetry, fiction, and nonfiction. The magazine's title is inspired by the huizache tree, a Texas acacia as thorny and tenacious as it is both invisible and ubiquitous, unwanted by farmers. Like its namesake, the magazine will promote fierce beauty that has been ignored. The voices in this magazine are motivated, not silenced, by harsh, unwelcoming conditions.
Publications Per Year: Annual
Submission Policy:
Accepts Electronic Submissions: Yes
Accepts Simultaneous Submissions: Yes
Accepts Unsolicited Submissions: Yes

Contact Information:
Huizache: The Magazine of Latino Literature
3007 North Ben Wilson Street
Victoria, TX 77901
Diana López, editor
huizache.prose@gmail.com

Illya's Honey
URL: http://www.illyashoney.com/
Publisher: Dallas Poets Community
Year Founded: 1995
Description/Editorial Focus: Publishes poetry
Publications Per Year: Biannual
Submission Policy:
Accepts Electronic Submissions: Yes
Accepts Simultaneous Submissions: N/A
Accepts Unsolicited Submissions: Yes
Contact Information:
dpcer09@gmail.com

Iron Horse Literary Review
URL: www.ironhorsereview.com/
Publisher: Department of English at Texas Tech University, Lubbok
Year Founded: 1999
Description/Editorial Focus: Publishes fiction, poetry, nonfiction, and photography every August, October, December, February, April, and June. Their issues feature a mix of established writers, relatively unknown regional writers, and up-and coming writers in all genres.
Publications Per Year: 6 times a year
Submission Policy:
Accepts Electronic Submissions: Only
Accepts Simultaneous Submissions: Yes
Accepts Unsolicited Submissions: Yes
Contact Information:
Iron Horse Literary Review
Texas Tech University
English Department
Mailstop 43091
Lubbock, TX 79409-3091
Lee Martin, editor
ihlr.mail@gmail.com
Phone: (806) 742-2500

The Lamar Journal of the Humanities
URL:http://dept.lamar.edu/englishandmodernlanguages/lamar%20journal%20of%20the%20humanities.htm
Publisher: College of Arts and Sciences of Lamar University in Beaumont, Texas
Year Founded: N/A

153

Description/Editorial Focus: *The Lamar Journal of the Humanities* is an interdisciplinary journal published twice yearly by the College of Arts and Sciences of Lamar University in Beaumont, Texas. Papers of interdisciplinary or general interests in the fields of literature, history, contemporary culture, and the fine arts are appropriate for submission. Languages accepted are English, German, French, and Spanish. Detailed studies of highly specialized topics, literary explications which do not elucidate broader historical or ideological issues and statistical essays in the social sciences are not encouraged but will be considered. Manuscripts, normally not to exceed 6000 words, should conform to the MLA Handbook or the Chicago Manual of Style. Two copies of the manuscript, along with return postage, should be sent to the Editors. The Editors will also accept electronic submissions if attached as WORD documents and scanned for viruses.
Publications Per Year: 1
Submission Policy:
Accepts Electronic Submissions: Yes
Accepts Simultaneous Submissions: N/A
Accepts Unsolicited Submissions: Yes
Contact Information:
Christine Bridges
Lamar Journal of the Humanities
Box 10023, Lamar University
Beaumont, TX 77710

Langdon Review
URL: www.tarleton.edu/langdonreview/
Publisher: Department of English at Tarleton State University, Stephenville
Year Founded: N/A
Description/Editorial Focus: *Langdon Review of the Arts in Texas* publishes poetry, short stories, essays, creative non-fiction, photography, and art. As a multi-disciplined journal, we hope that each issue demonstrates the diversity and varied creativity of artists who have a Texas connection. The main goal of the *Langdon Review of the Arts in Texas* is to provide a venue for the promotion and appreciation of the arts in Texas. We want to inform our readers about artistic endeavors that might have gone unheralded. We want to showcase writers and artists who have a Texas connection by publishing a considerable range of their work (10–12 poems by one poet; 7–8 photographs by one photographer, for example).
Publications Per Year: Annual
Submission Policy:
Accepts Electronic Submissions: No
Accepts Simultaneous Submissions: No
Accepts Unsolicited Submissions: No, only proposals
Contact Information:
Dr. Marilyn Robitaille and/or Dr. Moumin Quazi
Langdon Review of the Arts in Texas
Tarleton State University
Department of English
Box T-0300, Stephenville, TX 76402
langdon@tarleton.edu
254-968-9039 (English and Languages Office)

The Mayo Review
URL: http://themayoreview.blogspot.com/
Publisher: Texas A&M University-Commerce
Year Founded: 2000
Description/Editorial Focus: Poetry, fiction, non-fiction, drama
Publications Per Year: annual
Submission Policy:
Accepts Electronic Submissions: Yes
Accepts Simultaneous Submissions: Yes
Accepts Unsolicited Submissions: Yes
Contact Information: mayoreview@gmail.com

North Texas Review
URL: ntr.unt.edu/index.html
Publisher: University of North Texas, Denton
Year Founded: N/A
Description/Editorial Focus: *North Texas Review* is a yearly print publication that showcases the very best artistic and writing talent from among the UNT student body campus wide. *NTR* not only serves to highlight the minds and talents of students from all disciplines, but also serves to bring Art and English students together in mutual projects. *NTR* is published in the Spring semester of each academic year.
Publications Per Year: Annual
Submission Policy:
Accepts Electronic Submissions: Yes
Accepts Simultaneous Submissions: N/A
Accepts Unsolicited Submissions: Submissions are limited to currently enrolled students.
Contact Information:
Gwendolyn Edward, editor
ntrfiction@gmail.com

Overtime
URL: workerswritejournal.com
Publisher: Independent?, Plano
Year Founded: 2005
Description/Editorial Focus: *Overtime*, a series of one-story chapbooks, was created to showcase some of the stories we receive that are a little too long for our Workers Write! series, but are worthy of publication.
Publications Per Year: Quarterly
Submission Policy:
Accepts Electronic Submissions: Yes
Accepts Simultaneous Submissions: Yes
Accepts Unsolicited Submissions: Yes
Contact Information:
David LaBounty, editor
P.O. Box 250382
Plano, TX 75025-0382
overtime@workerswritejournal.com

Persona
URL: personaonline.weebly.com
Publisher: English Department at Texas State University, San Marcos
Year Founded: 1974
Description/Editorial Focus: Based in the Department of English, Persona is open to any Texas State student, graduate or undergrad. Art (photography or illustrations), poetry and prose are our interests. Our purpose is to stimulate the artistic growth of the student as well as encourage those with a creative flair to display their work.
Publications Per Year: Annual
Submission Policy:
Accepts Electronic Submissions: Yes
Accepts Simultaneous Submissions: Yes
Accepts Unsolicited Submissions: Yes
Contact Information:
Jordan Gass-Poore, managing editor
personatexasstate@gmail.com
Texas State University – San Marcos
Persona, Department of English
601 University Drive
San Marcos, TX 78666

Quicksilver
URL: academics.utep.edu/Default.aspx?tabid=55407
Publisher: University of Texas at El Paso, online
Year Founded: ?
Description/Editorial Focus: *Quicksilver* is a literary magazine published by students in the University of Texas at El Paso's online MFA program. Quicksilver has many connotations, both literal – the mineral was mined in Terlingua, south of El Paso – and figurative – the word means erratic, malleable. Quicksilver also equals charged writing: the best content we can find. *Quicksilver* invites quality submissions of prose and poetry from emerging and established writers.
Publications Per Year: Annual
Submission Policy:
Accepts Electronic Submissions: Yes
Accepts Simultaneous Submissions: YesAccepts Unsolicited Submissions: Yes
Contact Information:
D. Brian Anderson, Michelle Primeau, general and fiction editors
quicksilver@utep.edu

Pulse
URL: http://dept.lamar.edu/englishandmodernlanguages/pulse/
Publisher: Department of English and Modern Languages at Lamar University, Beaumont
Year Founded: 1959
Description/Editorial Focus: *Pulse* is a student publication exhibiting the work of student writers and is printed at the end of each spring semester. Entries are judged by an editorial staff and award winners are selected by a panel of faculty members with cash prizes awarded in each category.

Publications Per Year: Annual
Submission Policy:
Accepts Electronic Submissions: Yes
ccepts Simultaneous Submissions: Yes
Accepts Unsolicited Submissions: Yes
Contact Information:
Garry Richards, editor
pulse59@live.com

R2: The Rice Review
URL: r2mag.rice.edu
Publisher: Department of English at Rice University, Houston
Year Founded: 2004
Description/Editorial Focus: *R2: The Rice Review* is the premiere undergraduate literary journal of Rice Univer-sity. We are committed to publishing the best prose, poetry, creative nonfiction, and occasionals written by undergraduate students, as well as interviews with renowned authors. The journal was founded in 2004 by creative writing professor and author Justin Cronin and is published once annually, in the spring.
Publications Per Year: Annual
Submission Policy:
Accepts Electronic Submissions: Yes
Accepts Simultaneous Submissions: N/A
Accepts Unsolicited Submissions: Yes
Contact Information:
R2 Rice Review
Department of English
6100 Main St MS-30
Houston, TX 77005

REAL: Regarding Arts & Letters
URL: regardingartsandletters.wordpress.com/
Publisher: Department of English and College of Liberal and Applied Arts at Stephen F. Austin State University
Year Founded: 1968
Description/Editorial Focus: *REAL* is an international creative magazine dedicated to publishing the best contemporary fiction, poetry, and nonfiction. We produce two perfect-bound issues a year. Each issue is roughly 120 pages, and features quality writing from both established and emerging writers. *REAL* has published professional writers from all across the United States—and from Israel, China, Canada, Australia, England. Our writers have included the poets laureate of Oklahoma and Texas (Carol Hamilton, Larry Thomas), Mark Wisinewski, Ryan G. Van Cleave and fiction writers like Katrina Denza, Edmund de Chasca, Roy Kesey and Joe R. Lansdale.
Publications Per Year: Biannual
Submission Policy:
Accepts Electronic Submissions: Only through Submission Manager
Accepts Simultaneous Submissions: Yes
Accepts Unsolicited Submissions: Yes
Contact Information:

REAL: Regarding Arts & Letters
Stephen F. Austin State University
P.O. Box 13007, SFA Station
Nacogdoches, TX 75962-3007
reallitmag@gmail.com

Red River Review
URL: www.redriverreview.com
Publisher: Independent, online
Year Founded: 1999
Description/Editorial Focus: Our purpose has always been to publish well-crafted poetry using the best electronic means available. Our highest priority is the quality of writing. We will also post companion media pieces such as artwork, video the published poem being read by the author and other mixed media items that the editors agree are relevant. Again, our highest priority is the written word. Everything else is secondary.
Publications Per Year: Quarterly
Submission Policy:
Accepts Electronic Submissions: Only
Accepts Simultaneous Submissions: No
Accepts Unsolicited Submissions: Yes
Contact Information:
Bob McCranie, publisher
Info@RedRiverReview.com

Reunion: The Dallas Review
URL: www.utdallas.edu/ah/reunion
Publisher: School of Arts and Humanities at the University of Texas at Dallas
Year Founded: 2011
Description/Editorial Focus: For over two decades, *Reunion: The Dallas Review* has been dedicated to finding and publishing exceptional examples of short fiction, drama, visual art, poetry, translation work, non-fiction, and interviews. You may remember *Reunion* by its former name, *Sojourn*. We have a new look and a new name, but our mission remains cultivating the arts community in Dallas, Texas, and promoting the work of talented writers and artists both locally and across the globe.
Publications Per Year: Annual
Submission Policy:
Accepts Electronic Submissions: Only
Accepts Simultaneous Submissions: No
Accepts Unsolicited Submissions: Yes
Contact Information:
Editor, *Reunion*
c/o The School of Arts and Humanities
The University of Texas at Dallas
800 W. Campbell Road, JO31
Richardson, TX 75080
reunion.editor@gmail.com

Rio Grande Review
URL: academics.utep.edu/Default.aspx?tabid=65211
Publisher: Creative Writing at The University of Texas at El Paso
Year Founded: 2006
Description/Editorial Focus: Non-profit bilingual publication run by students of the MFA in Creative Writing at The University of Texas at El Paso. Accepts submissions of art (all mediums): photography, experimental texts, visual poetry, etc. Animations and audio files are, naturally, only considered for our online edition.
Publications Per Year: Biannual
Submission Policy:
Accepts Electronic Submissions: Yes
Accepts Simultaneous Submissions: Yes
Accepts Unsolicited Submissions: Yes
Contact Information:
Rio Grande Review
University of Texas at El Paso
PMB 671. 500 W. University Ave
El Paso, Texas 79968.
(915) 747-7012.
rgreditors@gmail.com

RiverSedge
Publisher: Department of English, University of Texas Pan American
Year Founded: 1976
Description/Editorial Focus: *RiverSedge* is a literary journal of culture and literature with an understanding of its place in the nation. Its name reflects our specific river edge with an openness to publish writers who use English, Tex- Mex, and Spanish and who discuss border life while not excluding voices from other areas. The Rivers Edge means many things: the edge of the Americas, divided by the Rio Grande, as well as the cutting edge of creativity in language and genre. *RiverSedge* exists to provide an outlet for writers of excellence in the genres of creative nonfiction, poetry, fiction, scriptwriting, visual art, and critical reviews.
Publications Per Year: 1 or 2
Submission Policy:
Accepts Electronic Submissions: Yes
Accepts Simultaneous Submissions: Yes
Accepts Unsolicited Submissions: Yes
Send submissions as PDF attachments to RiverSedge Managing Editor Robert Moreira: rpmoreira@utpa.edu
Contact Information:
RiverSedge
Department of English
University of Texas Pan American
1201 W. University Drive
Edinburg, Tx 78539
Submission guidelines:
Dr. Philip Zwerling, Editor in Chief
Robert Moreira, Managing Editor

Sagebrush Review
URL: http://www.sagebrushreview.org/Sagebrush_Review/SBR_Home.html
Publisher: University of Texas at San Antonio
Year Founded: 2007
Description/Editorial Focus: *The Sagebrush Review* is a literary journal published by the students of the University of Texas at San Antonio. We accept fiction, nonfiction, poetry, art, and photography submissions for our annual publications. We also hold monthly open mic nights to bring our audience together.
Publications Per Year: Annual
Submission Policy:
Accepts Electronic Submissions: Through the Submission Manager
Accepts Simultaneous Submissions: N/A
Accepts Unsolicited Submissions: Yes
Contact Information:
Sonya Eddy, managing editor
sagebrushreview@gmail.com

Short Story
URL: shortstoryjournal.tripod.com/Frameset/Frameset01.htm
Publisher: University of Texas at Brownsville, the State University of New York-Oneonta, and Claflin University, located in Orangeburg, South Carolina
Year Founded: 1991
Description/Editorial Focus: *Short Story* is an academic journal devoted exclusively to publishing the best of and about short fiction. It publishes original short stories, critical essays on many facets of the short story, book reviews of short story collections and interviews of short story authors.
Publications Per Year: Biannual
Submission Policy:
Accepts Electronic Submissions: Yes
Accepts Simultaneous Submissions: N/A
Accepts Unsolicited Submissions: Yes
Contact Information:
Farhat Iftekharuddin, editor
Short Story Journal
Submission for Publication
1817 Marengo Street
New Orleans, LA, 70115
fif@utb.edu

Southwest Review
URL: smu.edu/southwestreview
Publisher: Southern Methodist University, Dallas
Year Founded: 1915
Description/Editorial Focus: *Southwest Review* is the third oldest, continuously published literary quarterly in the United States. Publishes nonfiction articles, fiction, poetry.
Publications Per Year: Quarterly
Submission Policy:

Accepts Electronic Submissions: Yes
Accepts Simultaneous Submissions: No
Accepts Unsolicited Submissions: Yes
Contact Information:
Southwest Review
Southern Methodist University
PO Box 750374
Dallas, TX 75275-0374
Willard Spiegelman, editor in chief
swr@smu.edu

Southwestern American Literature
URL: www.txstate.edu/cssw/publications/sal.html
Publisher: Center for the Study of the Southwest at Texas State University, San Marcos
Year Founded: 1971
Description/Editorial Focus: *Southwestern American Literature* is a scholarly journal that includes literary criticism, fiction, poetry, and book reviews concerning the Greater Southwest. We look for crisp language, an interesting approach to material; a regional approach is desired but not required. We seek creative works that move beyond stereotype and approach the larger defining elements that, as William Faulkner noted, treat subjects central to good literature—the old verities of the human heart.
Publications Per Year: Biannual
Submission Policy:
Accepts Electronic Submissions: Yes
Accepts Simultaneous Submissions: Yes
Accepts Unsolicited Submissions: Yes
Contact Information:
Center for the Study of the Southwest
Brazos Hall
Texas State University-San Marcos
San Marcos, TX 78666
swpublications@txstate.edu

Story|Houston
URL: www.storyhouston.com
Publisher: Independent, Houston, online
Year Founded: 2013
Description/Editorial Focus: *Story|Houston* was founded to encourage and support developing writers in the Houston area and beyond. We serve the community by publishing quality literature for the general public, selecting work that appeals to a broad audience—anyone who loves a good story. Our online journal is the product of a dedicated volunteer staff, a highly credentialed editorial committee, and, most importantly, the many imaginative and talented writers who share their work with us. Readers, enjoy.
Publications Per Year: Quarterly
Submission Policy:
Accepts Electronic Submissions: Yes
Accepts Simultaneous Submissions: Yes

Accepts Unsolicited Submissions: Yes
Contact Information:
Robert Cremins, senior editor

A Strange Object
URL: www.astrangeobject.com
Publisher: Independent, Austin
Year Founded: 2013
Description/Editorial Focus: *A Strange Object* is an independent press based in Austin, Texas, dedicated to publishing surprising, heartbreaking fiction alongside thoughtful ephemera. We're talking about fiction that haunts and inspires us—big work that engulfs, that takes risks, that bucks form, that builds warm dwellings in dark places.
Publications Per Year: N/A
Submission Policy:
Accepts Electronic Submissions: N/A
Accepts Simultaneous Submissions: N/A
Accepts Unsolicited Submissions: No
Contact Information:
hello@astrangeobject.com

Texas Poetry Calendar
URL: www.dosgatospress.org
Publisher: Dos Gatos Press, Austin
Year Founded: 2004
Description/Editorial Focus: *Texas Poetry Calendar* is an annual print journal in a calendar format that's now in its 17th year, printed and distributed through Dos Gatos Press, a nonprofit, tax-exempt corporation organized for literary and educational purposes, seeking to make Texas-based poetry more widely available to the reading public and to support writers of poetry—especially in Texas and the Southwest.
Publications Per Year: Annual (ISSN: 1552-4698)
Submission Policy:
Accepts Electronic Submissions: Yes
Accepts Simultaneous Submissions: No
Accepts Unsolicited Submissions: Yes
Contact Information:
David Meischen, Managing Editor
Dos Gatos Press
1310 Crestwood Road
Austin, TX 78722
editors@dosgatospress.org

The Texas Review
URL: www.shsu.edu/~www_trp/index.html
Publisher: English Department at Sam Houston State University, Huntsville
Year Founded: 1979
Description/Editorial Focus: An international literary journal, which features fiction, poetry, scholarship, review, and creative nonfiction.

Publications Per Year: Biannual
Submission Policy:
Accepts Electronic Submissions: Yes
Accepts Simultaneous Submissions: No
Accepts Unsolicited Submissions: Yes
Contact Information:
The Texas Review
English Department
Sam Houston State University
PO Box 2146
Huntsville, TX 77341-2146
Paul Ruffin, editor
eng_pdr@shsu.edu

The Thing Itself
URL: http://ttijournal.org/
Publisher: Our Lady of the Lake University
Description/Editorial Focus: Publishes poetry, fiction, and nonfiction by writers at all stages in their careers. Mission Statement The mission of the journal is to publish the exceptional work of those who love language, regardless of tenure, experience, or genre. We empower a community of literacy and creativity both within our university walls and in the world outside. *The Thing Itself* is a print and online literary journal powered by the students of Our Lady of the Lake University. Until recently, the journal exclusively published student work, but has now opened its doors to outside submissions.
Publications Per Year: annual
Submission Policy:
Accepts Electronic Submissions: Only; use the widget here: http://ttijournal.org/submit/
Accepts Simultaneous Submissions: Yes
Accepts Unsolicited Submissions: Yes
Contact Widget: http://ttijournal.org/contact/
Blog: http://ttijournal.org/category/blog/

TORCH: poetry, prose, and short stories by African American Women
URL: www.torchliteraryarts.org
Publisher: Torch Literary Arts, Round Rock, online
Year Founded: 2009
Description/Editorial Focus: Torch Literary Arts is a nonprofit organization established to support and promote the work of African American women. We publish contemporary poetry, prose, and short stories by experienced and emerging writers alike. Our signature on-line journal, *TORCH*: poetry, prose, and short stories by African American Women has featured work by Colleen J. McElroy, Tayari Jones, Sharon Bridgforth, Crystal Wilkinson, Patricia Smith, and many more.
Publications Per Year: Biannual
Submission Policy:
Accepts Electronic Submissions: Yes
Accepts Simultaneous Submissions: No
Accepts Unsolicited Submissions: Yes

Contact Information:
Amanda Johnston, executive director / editor
3720 Gattis School Rd
Ste 800-197
Round Rock, TX 78664
admin@torchpoetry.org

Unstuck
URL: www.unstuckbooks.org
Publisher: Independent, Austin
Year Founded: 2011
Description/Editorial Focus: *Unstuck* is a nationally distributed literary journal based in Austin, Texas. We emphasize stories, poems, and even essays with elements of the fantastic, the futuristic, the surreal, and the strange. In our pages, you'll find everything from straight-up science fiction and fantasy to domestic realism with a twist of the improbable. Every issue of *Unstuck* includes a mix of established and emerging writers. Our journal is published each February in a big, heavily illustrated perfect-bound print edition. Issues are also available as e-books from online retailers like Amazon, Barnes and Noble, and (beginning soon) Weightless Books.
Publications Per Year: Annual
Submission Policy:
Accepts Electronic Submissions: Yes
Accepts Simultaneous Submissions: N/A
Accepts Unsolicited Submissions: Yes
Contact Information: N/A

Visions International
URL: visions2010.wordpress.com
Publisher: Black Buzzard Press, Austin
Year Founded: N/A
Description/Editorial Focus: We publish well crafted exciting poetry and translations from modern poets, everywhere. Particularly interested in translations from less well known languages. for example we've published work from Albanian, Armenian, Bulgarian, Faroese, Kurdish, Icelandic, Urdu, just to name a few.
Publications Per Year: N/A
Submission Policy:
Accepts Electronic Submissions: No
Accepts Simultaneous Submissions: No
Accepts Unsolicited Submissions: Yes
Contact Information:
Visions International
c/o Melissa Bell
6608 7 Locks Rd.
Cabin John MD 20818
Vias.poetry@gmail.com

Voices de la Luna
URL: www.voicesdelaluna.com/

Publisher: Independent, San Antonio
Year Founded: N/A
Description/Editorial Focus: Our mission is to publish a quarterly poetry and arts magazine with international flavor and a commitment to inspire, educate, and heal community members through the arts.
Publications Per Year: Quarterly
Submission Policy:
Accepts Electronic Submissions: Through the Submission Manager
Accepts Simultaneous Submissions: Yes
Accepts Unsolicited Submissions: Yes
Contact Information:
Editorial Office
14 Morning Green
San Antonio, TX 78257
Phone & Fax: 210-698-8785

WINDHOVER: A Journal of Christian Literature
URL: undergrad.umhb.edu/english/windhover-journal
Publisher: English Department at The University of Mary Hardin-Baylor, Belton
Year Founded: 1996
Description/Editorial Focus: The journal is dedicated to promoting poetry, fiction and creative nonfiction that considers Christian perspectives and engages spiritual themes. Each spring the journal hosts a writers' festival, inviting their published authors and interested readers to come to campus for a weekend of workshops and presentations on the connection between faith and the arts. We are looking for writing that avoids the didactic, the melodramatic, the trite, the obvious. Eschew tricks and gimmicks. We want writing that invites rereading.
Publications Per Year: Annual
Submission Policy:
Accepts Electronic Submissions: Yes–only through our submissions manager
Accepts Simultaneous Submissions: Yes
Accepts Unsolicited Submissions: Yes
Contact Information:
Dr. Nathaniel Hansen, editor
Windhover
UMHB Box 8008
900 College Street
Belton, TX 76513
windhover@umhb.edu

Writing Texas
URL: www.writingtexas.org
Publisher: Lamar University Press
Year Founded: 2013
Description/Editorial Focus: *Writing Texas* publishes the best fiction, poetry, and nonfiction presented by members of the Texas Association of Creative Writing Teachers at the TACWT annual conference; we also publish the first-place winners of the year's TACWT student contests.

Publications Per Year: 1
Submission Policy:
Accepts Electronic Submissions: Yes
Accepts Simultaneous Submissions: Yes
Accepts Unsolicited Submissions: Yes
Contact Information:
Submit and read at the TACWT Conference: http://www.tacwt.org/
Email the editors through the widget here: http://www.writingtexas.org/contact-us.php

www.ingramcontent.com/pod-product-compliance
Lightning Source LLC
Chambersburg PA
CBHW032012170626
46807CB00006B/2764